A Kind of Tragic Motherhood

Gem Burman

For Lauren, Harvey and Layla.

Contents

Prologue:

Screenshotting your crush's profile pic, then adding both of your photos to a baby generator app because you simply have to know what your kids would look like, even though you've never actually spoken and even though the result is always the same little Latino baby in the same pose no matter what photos you try – including your gran and Piers Morgan as the parents. We've all done it, haven't we? And now here I am, newly married and carrying his offspring for real! Who'd have thought it?

The trouble is, when you're busy whiling away the trimesters stuck in a blissful baby bubble, eating for ten and shopping for itsy bibs and Babygros, it's easy to forget that pretty soon you'll be pushing an actual human being out your vajayjay in front of a room full of strangers. Let's not sugarcoat things – that's the stark reality of it.

And with my due date fast approaching, I have to tell you that I'm absolutely bricking it, for more reason than one…

Chapter 1:

Then There Were Four

'Don't you dare let go of my hand, Dan Elliott!' comes the reverberating bawl of my voice, as rivulets of sweat drip down my fevered forehead.

'I'm right here, babe. I'm not going anywhere,' he assures, grimacing as my fingernails dig even deeper into his poor, maimed palm.

'You're doing really well, Lizzie. I can almost see a head!' cheers one of the midwives, staring into the lady abyss from between my legs.

'NOOOOOO! Put it back, I'm not ready yet!' I wail, earning myself some strange looks from the birthing team.

'Well, it's a little late for that!' The matronly, hard-faced lead midwife tuts with a not-so-discreet roll of her eyes.

'Can't I … h-have some more p-pain relief?' I wince.

'Lizzie, you've had gas and air, pethidine *and* an epidural. There's really nothing left to do ... other than euthanise you,' she says sardonically.

Bugger.

'Come on now, Lizzie, just a few big pushes and you're there. Would you like a look, Daddy?' suggests one of the other midwives.

Dan nods his head. 'Wow, yea—'

'NO, he would *not!*' I roar, dragging him back toward me by the hand. You see, if there was one thing that I'd made abundantly clear in my birth plan, it was that nobody but medics shall be allowed down the business end of the bed. I've often heard men liken the experience to watching their favourite pub burn down, but for Dan, I imagine once he sees *that* thing stretched to capacity in broad daylight he'll soon conclude that his favourite pub was beyond derelict anyway. I mean, it was never what you would call a pretty sight before all this, and I can't imagine that not one but *two* babies passing through it is going to do much for it on an aesthetic level.

Yes, two babies. As in twins. A terrible shock at the first scan, but since Dan and I are both in agreement that we wouldn't have any more than two children, it's a bonus that I only have to go through this bastard of an ordeal once ... well, doubly, but still only once in my lifetime. Mother has given her assurances that she and Dad shall be on hand to help out with the twins whenever we should need it – a bonus, I imagine, for most young families starting out, but in my case where Mother's concerned I'd say it's more of a penalty. We've already very nearly come to blows over baby names, and I can only imagine the uncurbed pontification to come over things like breast or bottle, dummies, weaning, potty training and everything in between. You see, Mother thinks the saying 'Mother knows best' was invented purely for her.

Dan's phone starts ringing for the umpteenth time. 'It's your mum,' he reveals, glancing briefly at the caller display as though we didn't already know it.

'Tell her to shit off!' I grimace.

'Goodness!' a midwife exclaims in surprise, as Dan looks on awkwardly.

Bless her, she hasn't the faintest idea.

'Well, y-you … don't-know-her-like-I-do,' I excuse in a series of breathless puffs and pants. If I know Mother, she'll be here getting on everyone's tits within the hour, so they'll find out for themselves soon enough.

'I'll, er, switch my phone off,' Dan mumbles, hurriedly burrowing it away into the pocket of his jeans. In the relatively short time that he's been son-in-law to Petunia Bradshaw, he's learnt fast that cutting off all communication channels is really the only way to deal with her type. Honestly, she's been like a dog with a bone ever since I reached my due date, calling every five minutes to ask if my waters have broken yet:

'Where are those grandchildren of mine?'

'Still in utero, Mother!'

'Well, they should be out of utero by now. They've been cooking in there long enough!'

'Oh, okay, I'll let them know.'

'Come on now, Lizzie, just a few big pushes down through your bottom and the first will be out,' the lead midwife urges firmly.

Clenching my teeth, I bear down and give it all I've got, letting out a noise that can only be described as animalistic.

'Now there's no use yelling like that. All you're going to do is give yourself a sore throat. Baby's not coming from your throat, baby's coming from your bottom,' she barks.

Is it really? Well! We learn something new every day.

'Push down through your bottom like I told you. Push, push, push!'

I glance up at Dan in desperation. He squeezes my hand reassuringly, right before the lead midwife pulls us apart, grabs my hand roughly and places it onto my thighs, knocking the drip in it as she goes.

'You need to grasp hold of your legs and push right down into your bottom!' she barks. 'There's plenty of time for all the lovey-dovey stuff later.'

Jeez, this is nothing like Call the Midwife. Why do I always get the militant types?

'That's it, that's it! Keep going, keep going!' she urges.

Oh, Christ. I'm not sure if it's working or if it's just a big dump! 'Am I pooing? AM I POOING?!' I demand, panic-stricken.

'Keep going, keep going!'

'Help! I think I might've fouled myself!'

Oh, God. Please don't let me foul myself in front of Dan!

There's a series of tugs, followed by a slither, then an enormous sense of relief from down below.

'Nope, you've not fouled yourself. You've got yourselves a lovely little boy!" the midwife announces calmly.

'Wait, I did it?'

'You did it, Lizzie! You smashed it!' Dan beams down at me.

Well, from the burning pain of my foof, I'm fearful that I very well may have smashed it!

Suddenly and without warning, I burst into

tears, overcome with emotions ranging from joy, relief, awe, disbelief and, as our baby son is placed onto my chest, pure unconditional love. The magical moments that follow will undoubtedly be the most precious in both our lifetimes as we stare in awe and disbelief at our first little bundle of joy. This tiny human being. Equal parts of us both. The most divine product of our love!

'Here he is, little Jeremiah,' the lead midwife coos.

A skip full of bricks crash-lands onto the grand piano that was playing epically in my mind. 'Er, Jeremiah?' I choke in outrage.

'Yes, your mum mentioned during one of her many calls to reception that it's to be Jeremiah for a boy.'

'Er, no it bloody well isn't!' I exclaim, appalled.

Jeremiah? Pissing Jeremiah?!

'Actually, we haven't settled on any names yet,' Dan quickly cuts in, leaving the midwife red-faced and apologetic.

Around ten minutes later, the urge to take a massive dump is back.

'Okay, Lizzie, same as before. Several big pushes down into your bottom and you're done and dusted!' she instructs.

Done and dusted? Sod done and dusted. I'm

about to become as far removed from sleep as is humanly possible; this is the mere bloody beginning!

I groan as I push, my face contorted.

'That's it! That's it! Keep going, keep going!'

'Gahhhhhhhhhhhhhhhhhhhhhh!'

'Not through your throat. Through your bottom! Your bottom!'

Somebody give her some laughing gas, for fuck's sake!

'Almost there, almost there!'

I roar in pain, two fingers up to the midwife, but before too long comes the same series of tugs and a slither, along with that same enormous sense of relief.

'There we are, now you've a daughter into the mix,' she announces through a stone-faced half-smile, placing our second bundle of joy onto my chest and invoking a torrent of sobs. My little girl! I have a little girl!

Holding our son in the crook of his hunky arm, Dan leans across the bed for our very first family selfie. Wow. It's as though I blinked and suddenly two became four! We're a family now; our own little family unit. My heart! I could cry … and I am.

Later, having been made comfortable – well, as comfortable as one can be when their lady-parts are on fire – and with both babies now fully checked over, family time is cut prematurely short when the delivery room door bursts open. A brief pause ensues, followed by a loud and highly pitched unpleasant squeal. What I initially deem to be some sort of drug-fuelled hallucination of Rumpelstiltskin – but is actually Mother in a sickly-green twinset – makes a mad dash toward Dan, lunging across the room to claim the babies and literally prising our son from his arms. Great. Up to now I'd had painful bits and painful boobs, and now I've a massive pain in the arse!

'Oh! The little angels, here at last!' she sings, without so much as a glance in my direction. 'Aw, look at you! Just look at you! All safe in the land of nod!' she coos, her beaky nose wrinkled up in delight.

Hm, perhaps not for much longer.

'Hello, Mother,' I greet her from my hospital bed, holding my little girl.

'Yeeeeees, hello. How are you dear?' she replies through a mad grin that's completely transfixed on the baby.

'Well, a little sore and—'

'Oh, that's good, that's good. Now, Daddy's outside, dear. He didn't want to intrude. Silly, I know, but you know what he's like,' she gabbles over me.

What, respectful?

'Shall I call him in, dear?'

Before I can reply one way or the other, she's striding over toward the delivery room door and summoning him inside anyway.

'Hello, darling. Are you quite sure you're up for visitors?' Dad enquires apprehensively from within the doorway.

Well, I was never bloody asked in the first place, but rock on.

'Of course. Come in, Dad.'

Maintaining her crazed grin, Mother proudly flourishes their new grandson toward him for a millisecond before snatching him away again. 'Isn't he a darling? Lovely colour! And would you just look at that button nose of his!' she trills.

Christ, it's a wonder he's not traumatised! I can't imagine what it must be like to leave the quiet, safe haven of the womb for the clamour and harsh bright lights of the delivery room … and what might as well be Pennywise grinning down at you!

'Oh, Lizzie, he's lovely,' Dad exclaims in awe, voice wobbling.

'I wish you'd call him Jeremiah, dear. That's what you were going to be named if you'd been a boy,' Mother blurts, clearly unable to contain it any longer.

Thank bleeding fuck I wasn't! I've never liked Elizabeth, but Jeremiah? Bugger me!

'I'd had my heart set on the name from day one, but you went and spoiled it all when you turned out to be a girl,' she complains, glaring at me resentfully as though I'd deliberately chosen my own chromosomes just to piss her off.

'You're having a laugh, Mother! We want a *trendy* name for our son. Jeremiah's crap!' I splutter in disbelief.

'Don't swear in front of the babies!' she gasps, moving swiftly to cover her newly born grandson's tiny ears. 'Well, I think Jeremiah is a wonderful name for a little fellow,' she insists obstinately.

'Bit old fashioned, love,' Dad counters feebly, earning himself a prolonged and odious death stare.

'Actually, we like Axel', I announce, looking over in Dan's direction who stifles a snigger.

'Don't you dare call him Axel!' Mother barks, completely taking the bait. 'Ye Gods! How could you even consider giving the poor little thing such a brutish name? Imagine how dreadful it'll sound called out in church!'

'Give over, Mother! Not all people get married in churches, you know.'

'I was referring to the christening,' she enlightens me.

I look to Dan, whose expression confirms what I was thinking. *What effing christening?!*

Mother shoots me a disdainful look. 'Oh, do stop larking around, dear, and hurry up and name this little chap.'

'Actually, I think we're pretty much settled on Jack. Right, Dan?' I prompt.

'Yeah, I like Jack,' he nods.

'Jack?!' Mother parrots in disbelief. 'Good golly! You couldn't pick a more common name! All you'd need is his father's name in the middle and he'd be Jack Daniel, like that trashy whisky!'

'That's not a bad idea, actually,' I half-laugh, leaving her with a face like a grieving pug.

'How about Aiden for the middle name?' Dan suggests. 'Aiden was always on the shortlist.'

'Jack Aiden,' I murmur in quiet deliberation. 'Perfect!'

'And what about for this little beauty?' Dad asks, stealing a look at his new granddaughter swaddled in my arms.

'Well, I quite like—'

'Aubrey!' Mother shouts over me, half-deafening us all.

'Pardon?'

'Aubrey, dear. Wonderful name for a little girl. It's classy, it's timeless, it's—'

'Crap!' I interject.

She's already lumbered me with Elizabeth for the rest of my life. I'll be buggered if my daughter's going to suffer the same fate with a name like bloody Aubrey!

'Well, what else have you in mind dear? Pfft, Tequila I'll bet!'

'No, no. I don't think we need any reminders of that bloody hen weekend,' I quip, silencing her with a knowing look. I look down at the angel in my arms and stroke her perfect cheek. 'In fact, I like Mia. It's cute for a baby, but trendy enough for a woman, don't you think?'

'Suits her,' Dan agrees, unable to take his eyes off our daughter.

'Lovely!' Dad declares, giving a nod of approval.

'Well, I beg to differ. On the plus side, I suppose at least it's a name that can't be shortened,' Mother grimaces, adjusting Jack in her arms. 'There's nothing more lower-class than a shortened first name, there really isn't!'

'How about Rose for the middle name?' I suggest excitedly, earning a tearful nod from Dan.

'Mia Rose. My granddaughter, Mia Rose,' Dad says, testing it. 'It definitely has a ring to it.'

Mother maintains a stark silence beneath her cat's arse pout. Observing that she's unlikely to give up her Goblin King-like grasp of little baby Jack anytime soon, I pass Mia to Dad for a hold.

'Ah, Lizzie. She's the mirror image of you,' he gasps, taking her from my arms misty-eyed.

Mother cranes her neck for a look. 'Goodness, we know who the heavier of the two is! *You* were a little porker, you know. That's why we were so convinced you were going to be a boy,' she remarks unapologetically, breaking her short-lived silence. 'But of course, you weren't a boy at all,' she adds, her tone laced with the same age-old disappointment.

The door squeaks open, and a midwife enters through it brandishing two tiny bottles of formula milk. 'Oh, goodness, we've a houseful! Who'd like to do the honours then?'

Mother's jaw falls open. 'You mean to tell me you're *not* planning to breastfeed?'

I close my eyes in exasperation. And so it begins.

Chapter 2:

Awks

Being in hospital with the babies was like being in a safe, cosy bubble, with midwives and medics on hand to help and give assurance over every cough, splutter and crying fit. I'd almost forgotten that the four of us would be returning to what was originally Dan's one-bedroomed bachelor flat as the long wait to buy our first home drags on. The plan had always been to get a mortgage with us both in full time jobs and *then* to think about having kids, but life doesn't always conform to best laid plans – something my entire adult life thus far is testament to.

'I'll get a better paid job soon, babe, it's just a matter of time,' Dan reassures me constantly, but even with the deposit we've had squirrelled away for a year, it'd have to be some salary to afford us a mortgage on anything bigger than the flat we're already renting. Consequently, until such time that I can get a job, it looks as though a place of our own is a long way off.

Still, if you wait for things to be perfect in life, you could be waiting forever and it doesn't have to be perfect to be good, right? We've a roof over our heads, we're all healthy, and as long as we have each other we can get through anything. People have babies all the time. *They* manage. I mean, truly, how hard can it be?

∞∞∞

First night at home. 2:45am:

Times woken in panic thinking have dropped babies: **22**

Paranoid checks to ensure babies still breathing: **31**

Thoughts given to the untold luxury of sleep: **incalculable**

Nappies changed: **4**

Bottles given: **8!** (Won't take full quota of milk and prefer to wake sporadically for ounce at a time!)

Current status: **fat and sapped!**

Somewhere in the midst of my comatose state, I'm aware of a phone ringing incessantly. I needn't be fully conscious to know that it's Mother's ring.

'Ughhh, switch it off,' Dan mumbles, burying his head into the pillow beside me.

I move to do exactly that, but there's always the cautious little voice within that worries it might be something urgent or that something terrible has happened.

'Hello?'

Damn you, cautious little voice!

'Ah! There you are, dear!' comes the shrill.

Where did she expect me to be at this ungodly hour?

'Now then, with life having gotten more hectic than ever for you both, I was thinking it would be a good idea to—'

'Call us at the crack of dawn?' I cut in sarcastically.

'Now you know how I feel about people who interrupt, dear! Pay attention, this is important!'

I sigh. 'Go on.'

'I was thinking it would be a good idea to get on with organising the christening as soon as possible!' she trills excitedly.

'The christening?' I parrot back at her, still half-asleep. 'Mother, I can't even organise taking a shit right now!'

'Goodness! Must you be so vulgar, dear?'

'Well, it's really the only language you

understand!' I reason, trying not to explode. 'And I must've gotten all of two hours sleep last night,' I add, the onset of daughterly guilt pricking.

'Well then it's lucky that you have me here to oversee things, dear.'

'You're not coming round?!' I roar down the line in panic.

'Stop shouting like that! *No*, dear, I meant the christening. I can plan the christening for you! Now, you know me and my reputation for holding a jolly good soirée. In fact, I believe it's my calling in life, I really do! Oh yes, I shall ensure a smooth-flowing, classy engagement – with the emphasis on classy, dear – leaving you both free to focus on the babies,' she sings all in one breath. 'It's the perfect solution.'

Chuff me! And here's me more concerned about finding a solution just to make it through the bloody day!

'Well, we haven't really thought that far ahead, Moth—'

'That's nice dear. So, I'll call the vicar and arrange a meeting, yes?'

'Whatever,' I reply, concluding that, if nothing else, going along with it for now will keep her out of my hair and, most importantly at this crucial moment with the twins sound asleep mere centimetres away, off the bloody phone!

With that comes the beginnings of a long, excitable squeal, cut short by a sudden click at the end of the line.

'Oh, she's gone!' I say with relief.

Away to hound the arse off the vicar already, no doubt.

'What is it? What's up?' Dan mumbles beside me, opening one eye.

I hesitate for a moment, the full realisation of how ridiculous it's going to sound at three minutes past six on this dark, autumnal Friday morning that is only day three of the twins' lives.

'She wants to plan the christening,' I relent, slumping back against my pillow.

'The christening?' he coughs, springing up in surprise. 'Do we even need one in this day and age?'

'Well, no, but she clearly thinks so,' I murmur.

He yawns, scratching his head. 'I didn't know she was religious?'

'She isn't. The only time she goes to church is at Christmas to watch the bloody carol concerts!' I explain.

'So, what's the point then?'

'She just wants something to plan, like most people who've got time on their hands and sod-all to do,' I reason.

'Can we even afford a christening, though?'

'What, with only your wage coming in and us not yet having even a toenail on the housing ladder?' I scoff.

'Well, surely you'd better call her and put her off then?' Dan cautions, worriedly. 'There's the four of us now and Christmas is just around the corner—'

'Not yet!' I cut in, turning over to steal another forty winks before the twins wake and start kicking off. 'While she's busy harassing the vicar, she's not harassing us!'

∞∞∞

Recalling the midwife's words during her visit to us this morning – 'you sleep when they sleep' – I decide in my infinite wisdom not to get some well-needed shuteye, but instead to make a birth announcement on social media.

'What are you doing? Don't go and wake them!' Dan hisses, wafting into the sitting room to find me arranging the blankets in Mia's Moses basket for the perfect photo.

'Just getting a pic for Facebook,' I mumble, opening the camera app.

'I thought you said Facebook is just a playground for the mentally unhinged?' he challenges.

Shit, did I say that?

'Well, it is, a lot of the time.' I shrug. 'But this isn't just a picture of someone's dinner, Dan. It's a birth announcement. That's the sort of stuff social media *should* be used for.'

'Well, it looks like your mother's already saved you the bother,' he enlightens me.

I freeze. 'You what?'

'Yeah, she uploaded a tonne of photos last night. Well, around fifty slight variations of the same shot, actually; her sat holding the pair of them in each arm looking mad as a box of frogs!' He chuckles. 'I thought you'd have seen it by now?'

'Pfft! I haven't had time to fart!'

'Well, Mia seems to be saving you the bother with that too,' he laughs, gathering up used baby bottles from all corners of the room. 'Honestly, some of the noises coming from that Moses basket!'

'Tell me about it,' I reply distractedly, snapping away on my phone.

'Christ, hurry up and get the shot before one of them wakes. How hard can it be?'

'Alright, alright! I'm only going to do this once, Dan, so it's got to be perfect!' I reason, moving on to baby Jack.

'Just take the fucking picture!' he jokes in a gruff, plummy voice, mimicking Prince Philip.

'These phone cameras don't do much justice,' I huff. 'If I get too close it gives him a butternut squash head.'

'Well, try it from further back ... and please tell me you're taking full, proper pictures and not just a limb here and there in sepia filter!'

'Of course they're full pictures! You know I hate all that stagy stuff,' I exclaim, quickly deleting the last five with a shady sideward glance.

As Dan busies himself cleaning and sterilising the bottles, I take to Facebook, balking when met with the sight of Mother's post right at the top of the newsfeed:

"Desmond and I are overjoyed to announce the arrival of our beautiful grandchildren, born safe and sound today and both doing splendidly! Meet Jack Aiden and Mia Rose, here at last! We thank you for your many messages of congratulations at this exciting time."

Bugger me, it reads like Buckingham Palace press release, and Dan wasn't wrong when he said she looked mad. Jesus, that grin would make the Joker jealous!

Just as I'm partway through typing my own children's birth announcement, Mia starts to stir.

'Could you see to her, babe? I'm up to my elbows in here,' Dan calls out from the kitchen.

'Just a mo!'

"Dan and I are happy to announce the birth of Jack Aiden and Mia Rose Elliott," I tap out. Hm, what else? Er ... *"Both doing great"* I add, before quickly hitting post as Mia starts screaming the place down. Damn, it's a bit on the brief side. Probably could have warranted a dash of baby-themed emojis to brighten it up a bit – a baby bottle here or a stork there, perhaps? Still, never mind.

'What's wrong with her?' Dan calls out.

'Well, I don't know. She's gone all red in the face,' I call back, peering into her Moses basket.

Before I can say another word, a fart to rival those of fully grown men erupts. It seems to go on forever, until finally there's silence.

'Christ, was that you?' comes Dan's voice from the kitchen.

'No, it bloody wasn't. It was the baby!' I say, unable to fathom how something that loud came out of someone so small and, although I am biased, beautiful.

'Yeah, yeah! Blame the baby!'

'It *was*! See, she's gone all quiet now. She must have a wind problem. I'll mention it to the midwife tomorrow.'

∞ ∞ ∞

When I'd agreed to Dan's family piling over to the flat to meet the twins this afternoon, I had been safely in my cosy new-mum bubble at the hospital – high on life and happy just to be alive and in one piece … just. The end of the week had felt an age away and I hadn't given much thought to my now permanently looking like shit – instead of just looking like shit most of the time – nor to my piss-poor form where meetings with the in-laws are concerned which, for some reason, *never* seems to go smoothly. Still, they're here to see the babies, not me, and there's no more a joyous occasion than a birth in the family, so surely two births mean double the fun! What could possibly go wrong?

'Ooh, little Jack's definitely got his grandad's eyes, don't you think, Danny?' Sharon coos, cuddling her grandson into her huge bosom as we congregate in the sitting room later that afternoon.

I inch forward nervously, hoping he can still breath.

'Er, maybe, yeah,' Dan mumbles.

'Nah! I think he looks the spit of Dan,' Dan's sister, Lucie, chimes in over Sharon's shoulder.

'He's got his nanny's nose!' Rob adds.

'Well, he's got his mother's chin, that's fae sure!' Crabby Gran mocks in her thick Scottish accent, shuffling over for a look.

Ugh! How did I forget that any invitation extended to the Elliotts would include that acid-tongued old bat?! And why oh *why* do people insist on giving their five-penneth's worth as to who the baby looks like? Newborns just look like babies, but so far baby Jack has Rob's eyes, Sharon's nose and my double chin, all while being the spit of Dan and, according to Mother, *her* absolute double!

'But Mummy, when is Uncle Dan and Auntie Lizzie's *other* baby going to come out?' Toby shouts, tugging on Lucie's sleeve and pointing toward my not-so-rapidly deflating bump. *Perhaps something to do with months' worth of gorging on Percy Pigs!*

'Don't be silly! There's only Jack and Mia,' Lucie corrects him beneath a fake laugh, the smile quickly dropping off her face as she makes desperate telepathic threats to confiscate the PlayStation. Hm, doesn't look like he's vibing though...

'But her belly looks just like Shrek's—Ouch! That hurt!' he whines, silenced by a hard, discreet pinch. Not bloody hard enough if you ask me, little shit. I've already decided that I'd never lift a hand to Jack and Mia in the name of punishment, but if Toby was my child...

'Matt and Laura send their best,' Sharon smiles up from the sofa. 'They really wanted to be here, but they're in Mauritius, of course. They both work so hard though, they deserve a nice holiday.'

'Pfft! They're never aff holiday!' Gran protests sarkily. 'That's the third this bloody year, by Christ!'

'Yes, well they can afford it. They're top earners. Work hard, play hard, that's what I say!' says Rob, rushing to their defence as he always seems to do where Dan's brother is concerned.

'Yes, and Mauritius was always on their bucket list,' Sharon adds, lovingly stroking baby Jack's cheek.

I glance at Dan, recalling the many items on our bucket list … well, more "fuck it" list these days.

'Awww she's so gorgeous!' Lucie coos from across the room, gazing broodily into Mia's Moses basket. 'You know what, I could have another of my own! Yep, I could easily have another!'

Please don't! Toby's already a pain in the arse enough, I have to force myself not to blurt in horror. 'Anyone care for tea? Coffee?' I manage pleasantly instead.

'I'll make the tea, you put your feet up, Lizzie. Here, Danny, you take baby Jack,' Sharon instructs, handing him over and springing up from the sofa. She knocks into my side with her enormous rack as she goes, causing me to topple face-first into Rob's crotch.

For God's sake, why can't people just sit down? I know she's only trying to be helpful but – and excuse my bluntness – I just pushed two babies out my crevice, so what's making a few cups of tea in comparison?!

'And hoo're the bairns sleeping?' Gran enquires gruffly, settling herself into a chair by the window.

'Sorry?'

'The bairns, hoo're they sleeping?'

I look to Dan to help me out of this conundrum. What on earth does she mean?

'Well, they seem to do all their sleeping in the daytime then come alive at night, Gran,' he sighs.

'Aye, well yer want tae put a stop tae all that early on before the wee beggars rule the roost!' she grunts, wagging a finger at him sternly. 'Jam a dummy tit in their wee yaps!'

'Absolutely not!' I explode, outraged, as Dan looks on in dread. 'It's lazy parenting!'

She peers across the room at me with pursed lips and frown lines deeper than the Pacific. 'Ge it a few weeks wi' nay sleep, hen! You'll soon hay yin in every colour!'

'Er, so then!' Rob booms over her, visibly

keen to steer the conversation onto more positive terrain. 'How's it feel to be a father yourself now, Danny-boy?'

'It's amazing, Dad! Words just can't describe …' Dan replies, trailing off as he tries to find the words.

'One of life's privileges, son. Gets you right here, doesn't it?' Rob agrees, thumping his chest.

'Pfft! Only thing parenting git me was high blood pressure, Rob!' Gran cuts in scornfully. 'Sharon was a wee shite as a bairn, ken!'

'Who's Ken?' I mouth toward Dan.

Rob slinks back into his chair beside me with a defeated sigh, and a glum, awkward silence ensues. Bugger me, to look at us all you'd think someone had just died!

In the moments that follow, I very nearly go on to die myself when Toby, having gone missing for a short spell, wanders out of the bedroom with his face covered in chocolate, brandishing what I instantly recognise as a now very redundant tube of Ann Summers chocolate body paint.

Holy shit! Perhaps nobody will notice—

'Whatcha got there, sonny?' Rob enquires jovially from the sofa.

Busted!

Toby holds up the tube and stares at the

branding for a moment as Dan and I exchange worried glances.

It's okay, the child is barely out of pre-school, he can't even read.

'It's Ann … Su-Summers … chocolate … body … paint,' he recites, his slow, loud and precise delivery making my stomach drop.

'Good God!' Gran chokes.

'Grandad, who's Ann Summers?' Toby frowns as Dan leans forward to try to prise the tube from his sticky hand.

'Er, w-what's this on the telly then?' Rob stammers, crimson faced. 'Shall we see if there's any cartoons on?'

Yeah, go on! Reward the little sod with cartoons!

'Look, everyone! I painted my face with it,' Toby announces gleefully as I try to exorcise all distant memories of *me* painting his uncle with the bloody stuff from my mind. Sadly it's not hard to do when it was so long ago, back when we used to fornicate.

'Christ, nay wonder they're popping bairns oot all over the place!' Gran scoffs from her chair.

'Gran!' Lucie hisses, wide-eyed.

'Well, it's true! Wi carry on like that gone awn, they'll end up wi a wee fetball team!' she mocks.

'So, Dan, how's work? Are you still looking for something else?' Lucie quickly cuts in.

'Er, yeah. I'm, er, looking for something better paid,' Dan pants, still grappling with Toby to get the body paint off him.

'Aye, ye's are gunna need it if ye's keep breeding at the rate ye's are!' Gran scoffs, relentless.

'Yeah, I need to get …' Dan goes on to add, trailing off as Toby escapes his grip.

'The snip!' she quips, unapologetically.

'Gran, please!' Dan sighs, eventually rendering her silent and stony-faced.

'Tea's up!' Sharon announces, breezing brightly into the room with a tray laden with teacups. She pauses, bewildered, as she's met with a blockade of glum faces – and one chocolate one – immersed in awkward silence.

'Look, Nanny! Look what I found in the drawer under Uncle Dan's bed!' Toby shouts excitedly after a brief pause.

Alexa, make this little fucker disappear!

'It's this cool chocolate body paint! Can I buy some with my pocket money, Mummy?' he asks, Lucie looking like she wants nothing more than for the sofa to swallow her up.

As I peer slowly around the room, observing

every mouth fall open in turn while Sharon battles not to drop the tray in embarrassment, I conclude that there are actually three cast iron guarantees in life: death, taxes, and being publicly humiliated by Toby.

I had thought that giving birth would be the hardest thing I ever have to do in my lifetime, but just getting through the rest of the afternoon comes in a very close second, let it be said.

∞∞∞

'How are we ever going to live it down?' I sigh as we settle down for another sleepless night.

'What, the chocolate body paint or your birth announcement?' Dan mumbles, scrolling through his phone.

I pause for a moment. 'What do you mean my birth announcement'?

'I mean the massive pair of pants airing on the radiator in the background on those baby pics. Didn't you spot them?'

'Stop it, Dan. I've had quite enough embarrassment for one day, thank you very much!' I sigh wearily.

'I'm serious. Look!' he prompts, flourishing

his phone toward me.

And there, just like he said, are my maternity knickers in all their glory.

'Oh, fuck. FUCK! Delete it! Delete it!' I yell, grabbing his phone.

Dan laughs. 'It's a bit late in the day for that! It's been up for hours and everyone's commented on it. You can't just delete it.'

'Well I can't very well leave it up, can I?!' I say, tapping away on his screen.

Dan leans over me. 'Wait, what are you doing?'

'Reporting the post!' I say urgently, scrolling through all the options.

'For what reason?!'

'Offensive material.'

He raises a brow.

'Well, it's not a lie, the size of those buggers!' I argue.

'I don't know why you're so bothered about it.' Dan yawns, reclining back onto the pillow.

'Because they look like they belong to an eighty-year-old, Dan. A very large eighty-year-old,' I point out.

'I thought you loved big pants?'

'I do, but I don't want it broadcast on social

media!' I protest, handing him back his phone. 'It's bad enough already, your family now thinking I'm some weird sort of chocolate-obsessed nympho!'

'You care too much about what other people think,' Dan mumbles. 'You'll never know how liberating not giving a damn is until you start doing it.'

'Well, I still don't know how we'll ever have the nerve to face them again.' I sigh, recoiling in horror at the thought of the next family gathering.

Silence.

'Don't you think?' I prompt, turning to find Dan asleep.

Pfft! And, to think that *they* think we're at it like rabbits!

Chapter 3:

Farmer Giles

It feels as though no sooner had I blinked than Dan's lousy week's paternity leave is up. I'm not going to lie, it's a day I've been utterly dreading.

'Babe, have you seen my car keys?' he asks in a bleary-eyed fluster in the front room.

The look I give him tells him I don't even know what bloody year it is.

'Shit, I'm going to be late. The gaffer's going to be really pissed at me!' he pants, tearing the cushions off the sofa.

'Yes, well, the gaffer ought to come and spend a night here himself. Then he can see first-hand how bloody difficult it is just stealing a moment to piss,' I reason on my way into the kitchen to begin frantically sterilising bottles and preparing feeds before the twins start kicking off again.

'Not helpful,' Dan replies, foraging frantically down the sides of the sofa.

'It's usually me who loses everything, not you,' I remark in surprise from the kitchen.

'Ah, bloody hell, I should've left ten minutes ago!' Dan panics, his voice rising in pitch with each lost minute as he scours every surface and tears through every drawer.

Shaking my head at the calamity we now call everyday life, I open the fridge and there, unwittingly, discover Dan's car keys on the bottom shelf beside the milk.

'Found them!' I announce through a smirk.

He skids into the kitchen, his look of hopeful anticipation morphing to one of equal parts relief and shame.

'Welcome to Club Twat!' I quip, thrusting them toward him.

'What are you both doing for contraception at the moment?' the midwife enquires breezily during her home visit later that week.

'Contraception? Don't you need to be having sex for that?' I remark in surprise.

Does this woman realise that there are times I've had to stir my coffee in the morning with a gigantic serrated-edged knife because there is never any clean cutlery in the drawers? And yet she assumes I'll find the time for sex. Meh.

She chuckles. 'Well, things might be a bit dormant in the bedroom at first, but once the twins settle into a routine, you'll soon be back to giving those bedsprings a hammering! A woman is extremely fertile after giving birth, you know. Once is all it takes.'

'No. Never. Absolutely never again!' I declare, shaking my head at the traumatic visions of the birth pulsing through my mind.

'Oh. That bad at it, is he?'

'What? Oh! No. God, no. He's a textbook lover, actually.' I smile, dreamily. 'What I meant was that I don't want to have a baby ever again in my life,' I add, dreamy smile dying an instant death.

The midwife bursts out laughing. 'All new mums say that. But if he's a textbook lover and you're absolutely certain there's to be no more, then it might be wise to sort your contraception, my sweet.'

Thinking about it, I can't remember the last time Dan came home to play with the box the kids came in, but, sleep-deprived or not, he's a man. It's only a matter of time before testosterone takes over.

With the midwife's scary warning still ringing in my ears later that afternoon, I decide to hot-foot it down to the high street just in case. I mean, shit, we need another pregnancy like a hole in the bloody head!

That sentiment is only further reinforced as I undertake the long process of getting myself and the twins ready and out the front door – Mia strapped in one arm and Jack in the infant carrier – downstairs to where we keep the duo tandem travel system tucked away in an alcove in the entrance hall, all put up and ready to go. With the clock running down to the twins' next feed, I don't piss about – well, other than when getting the pushchair down the front steps of the building, a ball-ache like no other, as any mum can bear testimony to.

'Christ, there's so much choice,' I mumble out loud, scanning the shelves at Boots to be met with all sorts of colours, types and flavours. Frowning, I spy an interesting looking bottle. Intrigued, I pick it up to read the label:

"Dr Nookie's Orgasmic Pleasure Gel. Turn up the fun a notch and turbo-charge your orgasm to soaring new heights!"

'Oh, it's Lizzie!' comes a familiar voice to my side before I can read on any further.

I turn in horror to see Sharon and Crabby Gran stood a mere metre away from me.

Sharon smiles pleasantly. 'We're in the area just picking up Mum's prescription. The chemist nearer us didn't have her medicine, you see.'

'Oh, hey. Hi! I, er...' I stumble, trailing off and quickly tossing the illicit pleasure gel over my shoulder in a panic before they see it and think I'm a horny bastard. Well, even *more* of a horny bastard! Luckily, I don't think they noticed.

'It's a wee bit late fae sheaths, hen!' Gran scoffs, gesturing toward the rows of condoms.

'Mother!' Sharon gasps, shooting her a contemptuous look.

'Oh, ha ha! I'm obviously at the wrong bit,' I excuse. 'I was just looking for the ... for the ...' My mind goes blank while the pair of them stare back at me, expectantly. 'The pile cream,' I blurt, naming the first thing I see on the shelf opposite. 'But it's not for me!' I add, realising they're now going to think I have piles.

'Oh? It's for Danny, is it?' Sharon remarks in surprise.

I stand gawping at her briefly. Well, if it's not for me and it can't be for the twins, then that only leaves Dan.

'Ye-yes. Well he, er, suffers quite a lot with them,' I add before I can stop myself.

Shit, he'll kill me!

'Well, he's never let on,' Gran frowns.

45

'Well, it's not the sort of thing you broadcast, is it?' Sharon chuckles, awkwardly. 'Anyway, how are the little cherubs?' she coos, peering into the pram.

'Ah, still a bloody nightmare,' I chortle, expecting them to laugh. 'A *good* nightmare, obviously,' I add when they don't. 'I think we've both forgotten what sleep is.'

'Aww, they'll soon start sleeping through the night. Then hopefully you'll get some,' Sharon smiles, causing Gran to have a sudden coughing fit. 'Sleep, I mean!' she quickly adds, flustered.

An awkward silence ensues.

'Aww, look at them both, sound as a pound! Better not wake them, eh?' Sharon whispers.

'Aye, we'd best get queuing fae that prescription, hen!' Gran barks. 'Cheerio the noo, Lizzie!'

'Nice to see you, Lizzie,' Sharon says with a smile.

Or *not!* Jesus, of all the bloody people to bump into down the rubber johnny aisle! Well, I'm not going to risk buying some with them still about. Sod it, I'm out of here!

Keen to avoid the vicinity of the queue for the dispensary like the plague, I scurry out the back entrance to the store leading out onto the next street. But just as I'm half through the automatic doors, an alarm sounds. I freeze – as does the lady beside me – then turn to see a tubby, middle-aged security guard with a beard already charging toward the door.

'I've only got a prescription, see?' the woman explains, waving her paper chemist bag in front of the security barrier.

He gives a stern nod and waves her through. She makes an alarm-free exit from the store. I attempt to follow suit, immediately triggering the alarm.

I shrug nonchalantly. 'It's okay. It can't be me, I haven't bought anything.'

'Hm, funnily enough it's usually them sort what tend ter trigger alarms,' the security guard mutters sarcastically. 'Could yer step back into the store please, love?'

'What for?'

'To be searched, of course.'

'But I've just told you I haven't bought anything, and I certainly haven't taken anything!' I huff, head wobbling in outrage.

'Well, you'll have nuffink t'worry about then, will yer?' he challenges.

'Here, check my bag! Check my bag!' I bark, flourishing it toward him. 'You won't find a thing!'

Well, he won't find anything from this shop.

He will find a few empty crisp packs and a random clothes peg, as it goes. Quite what the fuck it's doing in there is anyone's guess!

Satisfied that no stolen goods are hidden among the dreck, he hands it back and proceeds to check the pushchair.

'Er, what are you doing?' I bluster, anticipating the twins' trauma should they wake to be met with this brutish great lummox's puss peering over them.

'I'll need ter check the buggy, love,' he mutters, patting down the blankets.

'Hmph! Well, you'll not find anything in there either!' I splutter in disbelief.

'Actually, it's usually the first place we tend ter look.' He gurns. 'Oldest trick in the book!'

'I wouldn't know!' I hiss.

'Really? Well, what's this then?' he grins in delight, displaying a gob-full of overcrowded bad teeth and brandishing what I instantly recognise as the pleasure gel I thought I'd thrown across the aisle. What the ...? How? I mean how the hell is it in the effing pushchair?!

'I don't know how that got in there,' I squeak, heart sinking.

'Yeah, that's what they all say, funnily enough!' he mocks as passers-by begin to stop and stare.

'No, look, honestly! I'd only picked it up for a second to read the label, then I got startled when my mother-in-law spotted me, so I … threw it,' I explain.

'You threw it, did yer?! he chuckles, dubiously.

'Yes, honestly! It must've landed in the pushchair somehow.'

His face is telling me he's not buying it one iota.

'It's true, I'm telling you!' I plead, mind turning over daunting images of my public arrest. 'Look, she's still here. She's over there in the queue at the pharmacy with my husband's gran, see?'

'I'll speak ter them, but in the meantime you need t' come with me,' he instructs, full of his own self-importance.

'I didn't do anything, honest! It's just that … what with it being an embarrassing item—'

'Listen, it ain't a criminal offence buying fings ter aid yer sex life, darlin', but it is ter half-inch 'em,' he cuts in, draping a hefty arm around my shoulder and marching me and the pushchair off toward a side door.

'But I didn't half-inch anything! Look, this is all just a terrible misunderstanding. I'm a mature, married woman and mother of two with an unblemished past,' I chuckle in disbelief, wheeling my massive pushchair through the door into a small room furnished with a couple of chairs. 'I was actually just about to buy some condoms, if you must know! And that stuff just caught my eye. I only picked it up for a second to see what it was, and I got startled because I didn't want my mother-in-law and my husband's gran seeing me with it,' I plead in one breath, not that he's at all listening. 'Ugh, my sex life is already a family joke because we had twins. They think we're *at* it all the time and this would've just added to it all,' I go on, slumping into a chair wearily as the security guard takes out his walkie-talkie and mumbles a load of scary code words down it.

'Right, a female store colleague is goin' ter come an' search you while I call the Old Bill,' he explains turning to face me.

'You're not calling the police, surely?' I gasp in horror.

'It's just t'check yer record,' he explains, 'so if you'd like to pop yer name, address an' date er birth onto this notepad 'ere please.'

Taking a series of deep, calming breaths, I jot down my credentials and thrust the notepad back at him. 'I do hope we're not going to be here all day! The twins are due a feed soon,' I complain as he careers out the door.

Sometime later two female store colleagues pop their heads around the door. I instantly remember one from high school and pretend not to know her, but it's no good as she recognises me within all of three seconds of patting me down. 'Hey, ain't you Lizzie?'

'Um, well, I'm Elizabeth Elliott,' I tell her in a poncey, put-on voice.

'You *are* Lizzie. You're Lizzie Bradshaw!' she gasps. 'I ain't seen you since we was at high school! You remember me, surely? It's Cheryl! So, how are you? I mean, aside from getting nicked, of course.'

'Great. Great! Couldn't be better, thanks, Cheryl,' I say with a flush while she shakes out my shoes. 'Oh, but this is all just a misunderstanding, you see. I haven't taken anything. Something fell into the pushchair and set the alarm off as I was leaving.'

'Really? What was it?'

My eyes dart from side to side in perturbation.

'Er ... so how are you? Are you married? Children?' I blurt, swiftly changing the subject.

'Yeah, I've got two boys as it 'appens. Ain't married though. But *you* must be, what with the name change. Funny, I'd never have guessed you'd marry before me. What's he like then, this hubby of yours?'

'Well,' I chuckle, dreamily, 'let's just say I'm definitely punching. He's a personal trainer, you know. Amazing body! Looks a bit like that guy who was in the *Fast & Furious* films, you know, Paul Walker. He's the love of my life. Uh! Too good to be true!'

'Ooh, lucky you!'

'Right then,' the security guard announces gruffly, blustering back into the room. 'I've 'ad a word with this mother-of-law of yours and she says that she did bump into yer and that you was in ter get pile cream for your old man.'

Relief gives way to mortification as I glance toward Cheryl who is trying to keep a straight face, her mind no doubt awhirl with visions of some balding old git several years my senior sat at home waiting for his pile cream.

'No. No, that's not correct. My husband doesn't have piles. He doesn't, honestly!' I plead.

'Paul Walker, eh? Sure you didn't mean Paul Daniels?' Cheryl giggles. 'We'd better get back to work. See yer around, Lizzie.'

'He *is* a personal trainer, honest!' I insist, leaping to my feet.

The pair of them continue walking out the door, unperturbed.

'THE PILE CREAM WAS FOR ME! I'VE GOT PILES!' I shout after them in desperation, causing heads to turn across the shop floor.

Brilliant Lizzie. Good one.

Slamming the door closed in horror, I turn to observe the security guard looking at me, gone out. Making a brief mental note that it might be safer to keep my trap shut from hereon in, I slump back into the chair awaiting my fate.

'Right then. I've had a quick look through the CCTV and you can be seen clearly chucking the item over yer shoulder where it bounced off the hood of your pushchair and landed inside it,' he explains, a slight air of disappointment to his tone.

I nod in relief.

'And the boys in blue confirmed they've got nothing on yer their end … well, aside from you kicking off on a plane and yer ma being arrested for assault on two police officers some time ago,' he adds, looking me slowly up and down. 'This sorta drama runs in the family, does it?'

It doesn't just run in the family, mate, it fucking gallops!

'So, now what?' I shrug, blankly.

'Well, you're off the hook,' he replies in a slow, patronising voice.

'So, I can go, right?' I ask, springing up out of my seat.

He nods wide-eyed, waving a hand toward the door.

Grabbing the pram and releasing the brake, I make a beeline for it.

'Oh, and a word of advice to yer,' he grunts with a smirk.

'What's that?'

'Buying local's a good thing, yeah? But not fer yer kinky bits. Amazon Prime next time,' he winks conceitedly, tapping a finger on his punchable, bulbous nose.

Forcing a half-smile, I make a speedy exit, concluding that Amazon may very well take over the world, but for me, living in a sexless bubble is way easier all round.

∞ ∞ ∞

'What do you mean, they think I have piles?!' Dan very nearly chokes over dinner.

'Well … ugh, I didn't tell them you have piles as such. I said the pile cream wasn't for me, which only left *you*,' I cringe into my pasta bake.

'Oh, great! Bloody perfect!' he sighs, shaking his head. 'Lizzie, how do you get yourself into these situations?'

I only wish I fucking knew!

'Well, it's a common ailment and it's hardly a big deal, is it?' I reason after a pause.

'Well, yeah, I think it is! How about I call your dad now and tell him you're packing bananas?' he huffs.

'That's not quite the same thing,' I mumble in a low voice.

'Look, why didn't you just drop me a text? I could've picked some up after work, then you wouldn't have got yourself nicked in Boots and nobody would be sat thinking I've got bloody haemorrhoids!'

I pause for a moment, scouring the length and breadth of my foggy brain for an excuse that's playing hard to get. 'Well, even if I had, it would only be a matter of time before Toby comes across them in his next bloody scavenger hunt!' I retort.

Dan sighs. 'Lizzie, we've been through this. Toby's just a kid. Kids do stuff like that.'

An endless showreel of incidents caused by the little sod plays out in my mind. 'Oh no they don't, Dan. Not well brought up kids, anyway.'

'And what's that supposed to mean?' he challenges, slamming down his cutlery.

'Well, Lucie lets him run riot, doesn't she?' I snort.

'She's a single mum, Lizzie. She has to do everything single-handedly as well as hold down a job. Jeez, and you think *we've* got it hard!' He tuts, shaking his head.

I stare at him, momentarily speechless. *Okay, she's got it harder, but Toby's still a little shite.*

'I'm gonna go shower,' he mutters, leaving a scarcely touched plate on the table.

'What about your dinner?' I frown up at him, miffed.

'I've lost my appetite. Pasta's all we seem to eat these days,' he huffs over his shoulder.

'It's all we can bloody afford!' I shout in his wake, shaking my head in dismay not just at his overreaction, but at recalling all this started with an urgent need for condoms. Condoms, I ask you!

Chapter 4:

I Want it Now

'Don't forget you've got the gas boiler service this morning at 10.30 am,' Dan reminds me in an unusually downhearted tone, swiping his car keys off the sideboard and plodding toward the front door. He pauses partway through it and turns back to peck me on the cheek before leaving again.

Surely he's not still spoiling over the whole pile cream debacle? I get why he'd be embarrassed, but he said his piece last night. Christ, he wants to try giving birth for embarrassment; all your dignity goes out the window!

With the twins to feed, change and dress, the bottles to sterilise, feeds to prepare, the dishes to wash, the flat to tidy and then to somehow find time to get myself dressed before the engineer arrives, I shelve the issue somewhere in the hotchpotch at the back of my frazzled mind.

Just as I'm wiping down the kitchen worktops, the buzzer sounds. I glance at the clock: 10.10

am.

'Bastard, he's twenty minutes early!' I fume, slapping down the cloth. I mean, why arrange a time if you're just going to turn up whenever you bloody like? Those twenty minutes were everything – each of them precious gems with which I could've accomplished so much with the twins asleep … like getting myself out of these faded "I heart Prosecco" shortie pyjamas! Shit! He'll think I'm some sort of wino trollop still undressed at this time of morning.

Flustered, I tear through to the sitting room and trip over the changing mat, my left foot ploughing straight into the dirty nappy abandoned in a moment of not-so-clever multitasking beside it. Darting this way and that – and still wearing the nappy on my foot – I flap my way over to the door to answer the intercom.

'Err … hello?!' I yell in panic down the receiver.

A brief pause follows.

'Hello, it's Carl from the gas company. Here to do your boiler service?'

'Ah, you're early!' I remark through a forced chuckle, foraging for a normal sounding excuse as to why he can't come up yet. "Because I'm not dressed and wearing a shitty nappy as a shoe" is probably not the best one, though it's the bloody truth.

'Yeah, little early,' he grunts. 'But early's good!'

Er, no it bloody isn't, mate!

An urgent silent ensues until, having found myself at a loss for words, I whack the door release button and invite him up in a ridiculous squeak. I snatch a handful of baby wipes from the packet laying on the sideboard and hurtle off to the bedroom on one leg, frantically wiping my foot as I go. With mere seconds to spare, I toss the dirty nappy across the bedroom – will deal with later – tear off my pyjamas and grab the first pair of leggings I find screwed up at the bottom of my side of the wardrobe. With the majority of my tops still languishing in the laundry basket and soiled with baby sick, I grab one of Mr Organised's clean, hung t-shirts from the hanger. Underwear is simply out of the question. Still, he's here to service the boiler, not me. How is *he* to know I'm walking around pantless?

'Just a second!' I call out, throwing both garments on as a knock comes from the front door.

'Morning, come on in!' I greet him, opening the door in a put-on, sensible voice, as though it'll make me appear way more in control than I am.

'Morning,' he smiles back at me, but his smile doesn't hide the surprise on his face at the state of me. 'Oh! ACDC fan, are yer?' he enquires pleasantly. 'I would've thought they were a bit before your time.'

'Sorry?'

'Your t-shirt,' he says, pointing toward it.

I peer down at the large logo embossed in the centre of Dan's t-shirt that's straining beneath my massive bra-less bust and quickly weigh up my options:

> 1.   *I haven't put a wash on in forever and all my clothes are dirty so I'm wearing my husband's.*
>
> 2.   *Yes, I'm an ACDC fan.*

'Oh, er, yes. Yes, *huge* fan!' I lie, folding my arms and hoping that'll be the end of it.

'*Highway to Hell* was always my favourite,' he adds, jovially. 'What about you?'

I nod, staring back at him blankly.

'What's yours, then?' he probes.

'Er, well, I always liked...' I trail off, clicking my tongue and trying to recall anything at all from ACDC's back catalogue – a trying task when I've only vaguely heard of them! 'Er, "The Look of Love," I blurt, seeming to recall Dad playing it a lot when I was young.

Carl frowns. 'That was ABC.'

'A-ha-ha-ha! Yes, I know. It was a joke.' I blush, face going into spasm. 'Er... *Highway to Hell* is my favourite too,' I blag. 'Can't beat a classic, can you?'

'No, you can't,' he nods, looking at me blankly.

Oh, God. GOD! Of all the fucking t-shirts Dan owns, why couldn't it have just been a Calvin Klein? I didn't even know he liked AC-bloody-DC!

'I'll crack on then,' Carl mumbles, heading into the kitchen while I steady myself with some deep, calming breaths.

With the twins soundo, I take the opportunity to actually sit down and catch up on social media. Only once I am fully informed that Miranda Barnard has "cleared out the cupboard under the stairs and now making a start on the ironing", Kelly Grant is "feeling loved", Sally-Ann Wilson "just did a cheeky 5k" and Vicky Parsons "could, so she did", can I rest.

'Sorry, s'cuse me, love?' comes a distant voice, making me jump.

Flinging my eyes open, the gas engineer slowly comes into focus.

'All done for yer,' he announces, visibly trying not to laugh.

'Christ, that was quick!' I exclaim in a fluster.

He frowns, glancing at his watch. 'No quicker than usual.'

'Oh? Oh! I must've nodded off,' I blurt, flushing pink and springing up in my seat, hoping to God I'm an elegant sleeper and not the wheezing, unrefined great sloth I suspect I am. 'Er … I'll let you out.'

'No, no. You stay there, put yer feet up. I'll see meself out,' he chuckles, leaving me tense and blushing as I peer down and spot the hole in the crotch of my leggings, thoughts quickly advancing from *Jesus, do I actually own a pair of leggings without holes in?* to *Fuck! Did he see it?! DID HE SEE IT?!*

Only when I'm certain he's left the building do I venture down to collect the post where, tucked among the usual stack of bills, a formal-looking envelope addressed to Dan catches my attention. Ugh! Another job rejection letter. Yes, I've opened it. He'd been so hopeful about this one; really thought he'd had it in the bag. He's going to be gutted when I tell him he didn't get it.

'Perhaps I *shouldn't* tell him?' I think out loud on the way back upstairs. He's not himself at the moment and I'm sure it can't all be down to his family thinking he's got piles. No. It's got to be this job hunting lark taking its toll on him. He's bound to be feeling the pressure with the house situation and three dependants to support. Perhaps if I bin the letter and let him think they didn't have the common decency to let him know one way or another, then he needn't feel as bad about not landing it?

Before I can think any more about it, my phone starts spazzing out on the sideboard with Mother's ring.

Don't answer! Don't answer! Don't answer!

'Hello?'

Idiot!

'OHHHHHH, YOU'LL NEVER GUESS WHAT WE'VE GONE AND DONE!' she roars down the line, half-deafening me.

'You've applied to go on Gogglebox?' I guess off the bat.

'Goggle-what?'

Obviously not, then!

'Don't be silly, dear. No, we've got ourselves a little doggy!' she booms in a ridiculous, theatrical voice.

'You? *A dog?*' I very nearly choke. 'But you're far too houseproud!'

'Yes, well he's a corgi, dear. They're very intelligent. He has royal connections you know!'

'How could it possibly have royal connections? It's a mutt!' I gasp in dismay.

'He is neither an "it" nor a "mutt"! His former owner happens to be the Dowager Lady Jane Hastings,' she rebukes haughtily. 'Apparently, the Dowager was a regular at the Buckingham Palace garden parties before she went into residential care, and I'm sure with the Queen's mutual love of corgi's Horatio was simply bound to have been on the guestlist. Ooooooh, to think of all the aristocratic pats he might've had! Perhaps I ought to write to the palace to let Her Majesty know that Horatio has a new mummy?'

'I really don't think she would give two sh—'

'Now, *don't* swear, dear, not when we're on the brink of association with royalty!' She tuts.

'And what does Dad think about all this?' I press, knowing full well it'll be *he* and not she picking up Horatio's noble shit.

'Oh, Daddy's thrilled dear! The doctor told him he could do with losing a few pounds to help his sciatica, and with Horatio needing his walkies …'

An almighty racket of what I guess is doggy paws tearing across the hall accompanied by excitable barking ensues, before a loud crash follows at the other end.

'Desmond! Desmond, come quickly! I forgot myself and said the W-word!' Mother screeches. 'You'll have to forgive me, dear. I'm a novice learning on the fly, much like yourself with the babies,' she pants. 'And how are my grandchildren?'

'Well, they're—'

'HURRY, DESMOND! HE'S KNOCKED OVER THE UMBRELLA STAND!' she roars over the top of me.

Ugh, I give up.

'Good grief! We're going to have to do something about those doggy nails!' she wails. 'The prospect of losing the shine to my woodblock flooring seems to be bringing on a panic attack!'

'Look, Mother. I'm going to have to go, the twins are...' I attempt, craning my neck to see Jack stirring in his Moses basket.

'Jolly good. Jolly good. Yeeeeees, well I'd best be awf dear, Horatio's forgotten his manners ...'

'And so has his owner!' I remark as she slams the phone down without another word.

Jesus, Mother with a dog? I can't see that this is going to end well. But at least if anything it'll keep her on her toes and off my back.

Five minutes later, the former is immediately called into question when my phone pings with a Facebook message:

'Completely forgot to mention with all the hooha earlier, the christening is all booked. Daddy will drop round your invitation when he walks Horatio tomorrow morning.'

An invitation to our own children's christening ... how wonderful!

Days without sex: around 72 and counting

Daily thoughts about sex: at least 20 – all during starey bottle feeds.

Worries about Dan's search history: 145,000!

Ever since the whole pile-gate debacle, I've been obsessing over why it might be that Dan and I haven't yet resumed marital relations. The last occasion we did it – an awkward sort of morning side-spoon sometime during the last trimester – is all but a vague and distant haze … although jumping out of my skin and breathing in dramatically every time he goes to put his arm around me in bed can't be helping things much.

'I don't understand it. He's a man. Men have needs. Just *how* is he getting relief?' I shrug dumbfoundedly at Becca, my new mummy friend from the Little Owlets Mother and Baby group down at the community centre. As yet I barely know her from Adam, but nonetheless I have found myself discussing everything from nipple discharge to shooting vag pains … and now the distinct lack of shagging in my marriage. In normal circumstances these sorts of dilemmas would be offloaded onto Brooke, but since she's off travelling the world in a camper van with surfer dude Tom, it would cost me the bloody world in calls for the many occasions I find myself needing an ear these days.

'Well, I'm possibly stating the obvious,

chick, but he's probably polishing the banister.' She sighs coolly, jiggling the toy giraffe hanging from the baby gym her son, Noah, is kicking away merrily upon.

'Eh?'

'You know, giving himself a hand,' she whispers, raising a brow suggestively. 'I wouldn't worry about it though, all men do it.'

'NO!' I gasp in an opposing echo, possibly a little too loudly given the heads beginning to turn in our direction. 'Not my Dan. He wouldn't. He's too much of a gentleman,' I whisper in outrage, balking at the thought of him banging one out while I'm knee-deep in soiled bibs and Babygros!

'I wouldn't bet on it, hun. No bloke can go over two months not getting any. Pfft! My Jim can't even go a sodding week!'

'But what do you suppose men think about while they're ... polishing the banister?' I squeak in trepidation. 'Or *look* at!' I add, torturing myself with imagined visions of Dan ogling over-cinched Instagram baddies bursting out of barely-there swimwear.

'Well, I personally couldn't care less.' Becca shrugs nonchalantly. 'While he's off emptying his sack, he ain't bothering me.'

'But *I* want to empty Dan's sack!' I hiss louder than planned, as the majority of the hall falls silent.

Flushing pink and aware that all eyes are on me, I immediately turn my attention toward Mia lying on the playmat to my side. 'Ahh, are you smiling, bubbakins? Was that a smile for Mummikins? Yeees, it was! Yeees, it was!' I coo, willing the other mums around me to revert back to their ardent discussions about poo texture and projectile vomiting. Christ, even Mia's looking at me as though I'm a certified nutcase. What can I say? Going weeks without sex does funny things to you! They say that if you go without something for long enough, eventually you'll be okay without it, but that certainly hasn't been the case for me. I am literally Verruca Salt: I don't care how, I want it now!

'Er, what I mean is I *want* Dan to bother me. I miss him bothering me,' I go on, dreamily recalling the frolicsome poundings of yesteryear.

'Well, why don't you try spicing things up a bit?' Becca suggests, making it sound all so easy and simple enough.

'How?!' I bleat back like a desperate sheep.

'Well, you need to remind him what he's missing. Start walking around in your underwear and stuff. That usually does it!'

I give a shady sideward glance as scary images of me bent over in front of the television in massive pants filter through my mind. Jeez! I want to turn the man on, not give him nightmares!

'And spontaneity is key!' she adds. 'Don't wait until night-time when you're both knackered and fighting sleep; you've got to seize the moment!' She winks. 'Have you ever noticed that things you plan usually end up a disappointment?'

I nod frantically, mental regurgitations of my biggest ever fuck-ups and failures foxtrotting through my mind.

'It's the spur of the moment things you find you enjoy most. Sex is just the same. Honestly, next time you get the opportunity, just run with it!' Becca grins.

∞∞∞

While stealing a moment to actually wash that evening, I can't imagine for the life of me us getting an opportunity for spontaneous sex anytime soon.

Twisting to get out of the bath, I gasp out loud at the sight of myself in the bathroom cabinet mirror.

Voice in head: *Unless can somehow miraculously transform from vast deflated sort of shagged-out Mr Blobby suit to vivacious, yoga-loving waif overnight, then walking around flat in even sexiest of underwear likely to turn him asexual.*

Jesus, everything seems to have fucked-off

down south ... well, even further down south. And Christ, my belly button isn't just sad, it's downright disconsolate! Whoever has my voodoo doll, for the love of God, get it a gastric sleeve!

Ugh. Surely this sexless existence isn't the norm for new parents? Up to now, I've never had to worry about initiating sex, it just happened – often! So, what's changed? Might it be that Dan is just nervous about going there again after witnessing me giving birth not once, but *twice* in close succession?! Is it a lack of sleep? Money worries? Job stress? Has he gone off me?

Even though there are umpteen possible explanations I can think of, I've already convinced myself it's the latter.

∞∞∞

'HEEL! I ... said ... bloody ... heel!' comes a series of frantic, breathless pants at the other end of the intercom next morning.

'Dad? Everything okay?' I ask in concern.

'Not really, darling. H-hang on, I'm heading up.'

Opening the front door, I step back in surprise to find an excitable Horatio running laps around Dad's heels, death-wrapping him in the lead like a doomed bluebottle in a spider's web.

'GAH… duh …DAH! STOP it, you idiot!' Dad curses, stumbling this way and that as I scurry to unravel the lead, stifling giggles. 'It's not funny! We've only had the bloody thing for little more than a day and I'm already at the end of my rope with it!' He sighs wearily, limping toward me.

'What's the matter? Why are you limping?' I probe from under furrowed brows as the infamous Horatio trots in like he owns the joint.

'*That* daft bugger pulled me over chasing a bloody poodle in the park!' he sighs, clutching his back and glaring at the dog, whom I've already decided looks uncannily like Mother. It even shares her mannerisms with the way it stands looking down its nose at us.

'I'll stick the kettle on,' I announce as Dad grimacingly lowers himself onto the sofa. 'Are you alright? Do you think you ought to see a doctor?' I call out from the kitchen.

'It's more a bloody shrink I need, love,' he calls back. 'I honestly don't know how much more of your mother's carry on I can take. At our age, we should be winding down and enjoying life, but she doesn't sit still for five minutes! Always dreaming up these grand bloody schemes and roping me in!'

'*Oh?* I thought you were an old hand with all that?'

'Pfft! Well, even old hands have limits, love,' Dad mutters. 'I never even wanted a dog. This was all your mother's doing. How is it that I've ended up chief bloody dog walker?'

'I had a feeling you might,' I chuckle back while searching for two clean mugs.

'Ah! And speaking of grand schemes, I have your christening invitation here.'

'Hmmm, I kind of need to talk to you about that,' I confess, leaving the kettle to boil. I wander back into the room and perch tentatively on the edge of the sofa, taking the proffered envelope from his hand. 'You see, Dan doesn't seem to be getting anywhere with the job hunting. It's been rejection after rejection. I honestly can't get my head around it. But even so, moneys tight on just his wage. We've even started dipping into our savings for the mortgage deposit.'

'Oh? I had no idea things were that bad,' Dad remarks in surprise.

'Well, I mean, we're getting by … just! But we really need a bigger place; that's the priority right now. We can't afford a christening and, in all honesty, we were never bothered about having one. It was all Mother's idea!' I sigh, my eyes following Horatio as he sniffs every corner of the room. 'Do you think it's too late to cancel it?'

'Christ, yes! It's all booked, love,' Dad gasps. 'She's already had the vicar round for afternoon tea and half the bloody country club have had their invites. She's been out posting them daily.'

Jesus. How many is she inviting?

'Damn!' I mumble, 'Er... hang on a second, do you mean to tell me those toffs at the country club got their invites before Dan and I?'

Dad shrugs awkwardly 'Well, I assume so.'

'Oh, nice!'

'But don't you worry about it, love. You just leave it to me. I'll take care of the cost. It's always hard when you're starting out and you're right, your priority should be buying your first family home.'

'Are you sure, Dad?'

'Yes, love. Honestly! It is your mother's project, after all. She can't very well expect you both to foot the bill for all her frills and fancies.'

'Thanks, Dad. Oh, and don't mention to Mother about Dan's struggle getting better paid work, will you? You know how pompous she is. She'll just assume it's him being incompetent. But it's not his fault, Dad. He's better than that.'

'I know he is, love. He's a grafter is your Dan. Something will turn up for him soon, you'll see.'

The appreciative smile on my face soon begins to drop as I slide out the invitation from the luxury, premium envelope, complete with ornate wax seal, and begin reading the pretentious metallic gold wording.

'Jesus, all it's missing is the royal bloody crest!' I gulp.

Dad rolls his eyes empathetically.

'Oh! It says here the reception is to be held at yours?' I remark in surprise.

'She wants to show off the new conservatory,' he groans, shaking his head.

I freeze open-mouthed, consumed with dread at the prospect of Mother hosting both sides of Dan and I's families. I mean, I'm no Nostradamus, but all those big characters clashing within an intimate space? It's got "fucking disaster" written all over it!

'Are you okay, love? You seem to have lost your colour,' Dad frowns, going on to lose his own as we both glance across the room just in time to see Horatio cocking his leg and pissing up the side of the sofa.

Chapter 5:

Drunkle Tony

Dan: *Just a gentle reminder that it's Dad's 60th tonight x*

Me: *Knew that! x*

Dan: *Was just in case you were having one of your moments x*

Me: *My entire life has been one great moment! x*

Dan: *True. See you tonight. Pls be ready on time! x*

Me: *Of course! What do you take me for?! x*

Four hours later

Outfit: *Wardrobe chaotic, yet fuck-all to wear.*

Hair: *Would make Mad Hatter envious.*

Make-up: *Maybe it's the lack of skill, maybe it's Maybelline!*

Shoes: *Like Cinderella, can only locate one of.*

Bollocks, bollocks, bollocks! This is all very inconvenient! Bloody Rob! Why does his birthday have to be today? Why couldn't it have been in spring, by which time I'm far more likely to have my shit together? Hm, don't actually think I've *ever* had my shit together. Ugh.

'Lizzie, we need to leave now. Like, *right* now!' Dan prompts anxiously from the front room. 'We should've left twenty minutes ago!'

'I know! I'm coming!' I screech like a banshee, having one last frantic check of my appearance in the mirrored wardrobe doors. Well, I'm not at my best, but at least my hair's clean, *I'm* clean and I don't smell of baby sick. *That's probably about the best I can expect*, I think to myself, smoothing down my ditsy floral wrap dress.

'I knew we'd be late,' Dan moans out at the car, giving the straps on Jack's car seat a final tug before quickly closing the rear passenger door, clambering into the driver's seat and making a weird attempt to pull away at speed without even having started the engine. He glances at me sheepishly, shakes his head and says nothing.

During the journey to Dan's parents' house, my thoughts merge into one giant tapestry of anxiety:

Did I unplug the hair straighteners?

The flat could very well be burning to the ground as we speak!

Dan usually compliments me when I get dressed-up, but he didn't tonight.

Do I look that bad?

Do I embarrass him?

We still haven't slept together!

Oh, fuck! I've got to face Sharon and that sarky old bat for the first time since Boots. The whole family is bound to know I was nicked by security!

And what about the chocolate body paint incident?!

I know they don't like me!

I bet they're already sat around slagging me off!

As we approach the house, visibly bustling with party guests and cars crammed on every verge in the near vicinity, my nerves rev up a gear.

Voice in head: *Just get inside, greet them with pleasant small talk, then find the gin!*

'Hello, soldier!' Sharon beams, answering the door in a spangly bodycon sequin dress far more at home on a twenty-five-year-old.

'Hey, Mum!'

'Awwwwww, there they are, the little bobbins. Look at them, wide awake!' she coos, peering down into the car seats either side of Dan's feet. 'They're changing already!' she adds in a dramatic gasp, tickling Mia's cheek.

'You think so?' Dan smiles, proudly.

'Yes, you're growing far too quickly, aren't you my ickle, wickle, itsy, witsy baby boos!'

Jesus.

'Come in then! We've got a bit of a housefull, so I've put Norbert outside out of the way,' Sharon explains.

Thank fuck for that!

'He just gets too boisterous around people and we're fighting for space as it is!' she adds, reaching for Mia's car seat.

Pfft! Ain't that the truth, I think to myself, picturing those offensive, great balls. Why anyone would willingly choose such an enormous rampant hound for a pet is beyond me.

'Oh, hello Lizzie, how are you?' Sharon finally greets me, eyes dipping downward in assessment of my outfit, her expression visibly irked at the dire lack of spangle.

'Hi, Sharon. I'm good thanks. You?'

'Oh, Danny! You *have* to see Matt and Laura's holiday pics. AGH! You should see the hotel they stayed in. Five-star! Absolute heaven! I said to your dad, I said "Rob, it's high time we did the same". None of us are getting any younger, are we?' she yatters manically, grabbing Mia's car seat and ushering Dan inside.

Alright then, don't answer, I think to myself, following awkwardly behind like some *persona non grata*.

'Watchaaa, Danny-boy!' comes a hyperactive boom to our left, instantly recognisable as Uncle Tony's – Rob's unmarried younger brother and chief *persona non grata* who has acquired the secret nickname Drunkle Tony on account of his love of the booze. I've only met him the once, briefly, but Christ you don't forget someone like him easily, let me tell you that.

'Oh hey, U.T,' Dan greets him, shaking his hand politely with a put-on smile.

Suddenly, I don't feel half as self-conscious as I observe Uncle Tony already staggering around with glassy eyes and an insane grin, earning himself some pretty contemptuous looks from various onlookers. Uh, how refreshing not to be the outcast for once, though? I reckon this might turn out to be a decent night after all!

'Ow's mawwied life tweatin' yer, then?' Uncle Tony grins, throwing his arm around Dan's shoulder and very nearly pulling him into the towering potted cheese plant stood at the side of the door.

'Er, good! Good, thanks!' Dan stammers, struggling to stay upright.

'Nevvver understood why people wush off ter get 'itched,' Uncle Tony slurs in Dan's face,

'Nuffin worse than bein' tied down, eh?'

'Well, not if you find the one,' Dan chuckles awkwardly, veering backwards in the fight to defend his personal space.

'Alweady found 'er, mate. She's called bwandy!' Uncle Tony guffaws, holding out his near-empty glass with a crazed wink.

Mental notes:

Dan still thinks I'm 'the one'!

Uncle Tony's flies are undone.

'I've got your bed and both travel cots all made up in the back room. Just take the bobbins up whenever they're ready for beddy-byes,' Sharon coos, perfectly ignoring Uncle Tony and whisking Mia from her car seat. 'Here y'are, Shirl! Come and meet Dan's little 'uns!' She grins, as Auntie Shirley breezes out of the downstairs loo in a toxic cloud of Thierry Mugler.

'Ooh, just look at those chubby cheeks! Coochy-coo! Coochy-coo!' she screeches rabidly, swiping a disconcerted-looking Jack from his car seat, lifting him to her massive knockers and smothering him with kisses, besmearing the poor soul with her brash, eighties-pink lipstick.

I shoot Dan a worried-parent look, to which he makes a gesture that all is well and Auntie Shirley is not about to eat our son.

'Could we get a drink?' I mumble.

'Sure, come on. The twins are fine with Mum and Auntie Shirl,' Dan replies, ushering me through the hallway.

Glancing over my shoulder apprehensively, I observe Auntie Shirley making deranged faces at Jack, whose bottom lip begins quivering in readiness to scream the place down. 'Um, Dan, I think he's going to cry,' I gasp, pointing worriedly over my shoulder.

'Oh, *he's* alright,' he dismisses with a casual shrug.

Auntie Shirley turns toward us, staunchly refusing to give up Jack from the clutches of her neon talons, even though it's obvious he's traumatised. 'Yes! you've gotta let him mix with people what he don't know. You don't want him strange!'

Strange, she says? That's a laugh!

'It's fine, honestly, just relax! Come on, let's enjoy ourselves,' Dan urges, coaxing me off toward the kitchen.

'Ah! Hello, guys!' Rob greets us, pulling us into a group hug. 'Great to see you both!'

'Happy sixtieth!' we greet him collectively.

'Hm, yes. Another bloody year older,' he grunts despondently.

'Well, at least you're not as old as you will

be next year,' I blurt in a failed attempt to reassure him.

He shoots me a strange look. 'Yes, thank you Lizzie. Er, help yourselves to food and drink.'

'Cheers, Dad.'

'Mine's a Jack Daniels and Coke,' I mutter to Dan. 'Better make it a double, and go easy on the Coke,' I add, spying Crabby Gran over at the buffet table to my right with a face like a robber's dog.

'A double? Are you sure that's wise?' Dan frowns back at me.

I let my expression do the talking.

'Okay, okay! You're *not* my child. You can handle your drink, *etcetera, etcetera,*' he mutters, reading me perfectly. He turns back toward me suddenly, glancing down at my neckline. 'Very nice,' he mutters with a slight smirk.

'What, this old thing?' I remark in surprise, gesturing towards my dress.

'Well, more the cracking boobs underneath it,' he says with a chuckle.

'Naughty!' I laugh, bashfully.

'Shame we're staying over tonight,' he adds after a prolonged pause, plopping an ice cube into my glass.

Wait … are we flirting?!

'Oh? Why's that then?' I probe, making

saucy eyes at him.

'Well, you're getting me going, aren't you?' he mumbles, discreetly. 'Would've been nice to take you home and—'

'Bro! How you doing?!' Matt interrupts, slapping Dan on the back and bringing about an immediate end to that rare, fifteen-second horny exchange.

Ugh!

'Hi, Laura. You're looking very tanned!' I smile sweetly on her approach while Dan and Matt get lost in brotherly conversation.

'Well, yes! Even at this time of year the climate in Mauritius is so hot!' She sighs, overweeningly. 'But I don't think Matt and I would have it any other way. We just love to travel.'

I force a smile, already bored shitless with the holiday talk and my mind conjuring explicit scenes of Dan and I's rampant lovemaking. Ugh, of all the times he could've given me the come-on!

'I suppose it'll be a while before you and Dan manage it,' Laura adds.

Hm, not half!

'Yes, it's been ages,' I reply through gritted teeth.

'Well, I'm sure you'll be able to grab a package once the kids are a bit older,' she smiles.

I nod politely, eyes lingering upon the only package I want to grab.

'Laura! God, you look amazing!' Lucie exclaims dramatically on her way over to join us. 'Mum showed us the holiday pics. Agh! So jealous!' She sighs. 'Oh, hi, Lizzie.'

'Hiya.'

Suddenly alerted to the heightening screams of my offspring from the hallway, I put my drink down on the countertop, leaving the pair of them embroiled in conversation about the Piton de la Petite Riviere Noire.

'I think he's done a poo!' Auntie Shirley grimaces, suspending a visibly anxious Jack in mid-air as though he were diseased.

Well, you will insist on grinning at him with those teeth...

'Actually, I ought to be getting them up to bed, anyway,' I smile, taking him from her. 'They were fed just before we left. I thought they'd nod off in the car, but they didn't, so they're probably ready to go down now.'

'Alright hun, you take Jack and I'll take—' Sharon begins.

'I'll take Mia!' Dan cuts in urgently from behind me.

I turn and glance at him over my shoulder. He looks back at me with hungry eyes. Hm, weird.

I thought I'd lost him to Matt for the evening?

OMG, HE WANTS TO GET ME ALONE! SPON-TANEOUS SEX!

'I remember when *you* was his age,' Auntie Shirley smiles pensively at Dan, blocking the stair-case.

'Oh really?' he remarks, scooping up Mia.

'Hm, yes. Remember it like it was yesterday.'

He nods, not quite sure what else to say.

'Well, er, we'd best be getting upstairs then' I smile, nether regions convulsing.

'Scary how they grow up so quick, ain't it?' Auntie Shirley muses in a robotic tone.

'Yes, isn't it?' I agree, pushing past her.

Out the way biatch, I'm on a promise!

Laying Jack on the bed to give him the quick-est nappy change of his life thus far, Becca's words replay in my mind: 'next time you get the chance, just run with it!' But, here, at the in-laws'?

'Oh, Jack hasn't pooed at all!' I remark in sur-prise, finding his nappy clean.

'Mia's clean too,' Dan adds, placing her down into her cot.

'Oh? What on earth was Auntie Shirley smelling, then?'

As I lean over to put Jack down in his cot,

Dan places a hand on my backside, prompting me to pause, an endorsing smile creeping up my face.

'Come here,' he whispers, grabbing me by the hips.

Throwing caution to the wind, I spin around and we begin kissing urgently, hands wandering, pulses racing. Enveloped in Dan's strong arms, knees weakening at the masculine spice of his aftershave, I conclude that right now there is no place I would rather be. Well, other than for our own bedroom, of course.

'Dan,' I pant, breathlessly.

'Yeah?'

'Have you got a ... thingie?'

'Yeah, I've had one since checking out your boobs in the kitchen earlier,' he moans.

'No, not that! I meant a condom.'

'Oh, er, yeah. Put one in my washbag, just in case,' he mumbles, 'I'll just grab it.'

Wow, how is this man being rejected for jobs left, right and centre with initiative like that?!

'Is the door locked?' I ask as he rifles through his overnight bag.

'No, there's no lock.'

'Could you maybe ... wedge a chair under it, then?' I sigh, visions of someone taking the wrong door to the bathroom unnerving me.

'What chair?'

I glance around the room to find it significantly lacking in chairs.

'Turn the light off then?' I suggest.

Any angst I might've felt about my colossal pants is immediately diminished as he moves toward the door, plunging us into darkness. Lunging back toward me, he pushes me onto the bed, yanking my dress up around my waist. Jesus, one minute we were lost in a barren sexual wasteland, and the next we're going at it like the clappers!

'Oh my God, Dan, yes!' I moan in his ear, completely lost in the moment.

Becca was so right; spontaneous sex is where it's at!

∞∞∞

'Ah, you're just in time. We're about to do the birthday cake,' Sharon greets us as we venture into the packed front room with everyone poised and ready to sing.

'Did the twins go down alright?' Auntie Shirley probes.

'Well, they took a bit of settling,' Dan excuses, giving me a side-glance. 'We were just giving them both a top-up bottle.'

'No, you weren't!' comes a juvenile voice from the doorway.

We both turn to see Toby stood in dinosaur pyjamas, grinning from ear to ear.

'You were on top of Auntie Lizzie!' he accuses loudly, pointing his finger at Dan.

Uncle Tony roars with laughter, giving Dan a congratulatory slap on the back. 'Was you up there getting yer end away, lad?'

'Don't be daft! Course, I wasn't!' Dan chuckles nervously, while I slowly curl up and die.

'And his bum was going up and down, like this!' Toby adds, going on to demonstrate with his toy robot, sending Uncle Tony into hysterics while sniggers erupt from all corners of the room.

Okay, I officially wish to throttle this child!

'Christ, can you pair nay keep yer hands aff each other fe five minutes?' Crabby Gran scoffs, adding insult to injury.

'TOBY! Right, that's it! Get back upstairs to bed!' Lucie hisses as I stand there trying to look busy, the way newsreaders always do as the camera pans out at the end of the programme.

'Too late, love. Horse has alweady bolted,' Uncle Tony laughs.

'Right then! Er...er, happy birthday to yooou...' Sharon prompts stiffly as Matt walks in with the cake looking puzzled.

I glance up at Dan, who's face you could fry an egg on – much like my own – and we begrudgingly launch into half-arsed song, trying to avoid eye contact with everyone.

'You, ok?' Dan asks, walking into the kitchen later in the evening to find me necking straight whisky.

'What, now the entire place knows we were upstairs shagging? Yeah, bloody dandy!' I mutter.

'I didn't even realise he was here. I thought he was with a babysitter or something,' Dan gasps in wide-eyed disbelief. 'And I never heard the door open, did you?'

'No, not even a squeak,' I proclaim with a hiccup as the booze starts to hit. 'Look, Dan. I really don't think I can stay here tonight. Not after this,' I tell him, perishing the thought of being savaged over the breakfast table by a certain acid-tongued pensioner in the morning.

Before he can answer, Uncle Tony crashes into the kitchen, smashing bottles off the worktop and belting out a slurry, incoherent rendition of "Take Me Home, Countwy Woads".

'I wish somebody would bloody well take him home!' tuts an unknown hard-faced woman to my right.

'Commme on everyone, come onnnnnn!' he

roars, grabbing said hard-faced woman by the waist and forcing her into a gropey waltz.

'Rob, I think you'd best call Tony a cab before somebody hits him,' Sharon gasps, ashen faced.

'I can call him a cab easily enough, darling. It's getting him in it that's going to pose a problem,' Rob grimaces, wincing as Uncle Tony receives a well-earned slap around the chops.

'Well, that's charrrming, innit?' he slurs, rubbing at his cheek. 'Bloody wommmen, all the same!'

'Rob, call that sodding cab for Christ's sake!' Sharon growls, closing her eyes in exasperation. 'You *know* what happened last time!'

Intriguing!

'What happened last time?' I whisper to Dan.

'You don't want to know, it's pretty gross,' he replies, making a disgusted expression.

'No, come on, I take great comfort from these things. Spill!' I persist, poking him in the ribs.

'Ugh, alright,' he grunts, rolling his eyes. 'Uncle Tony sometimes loses control of his bowels when he's been on a bender,' he explains, discreetly. 'To cut a long story short, he shat himself at Dad's fiftieth. Ruined the three-piece suite. Mum was livid!'

'No way!' I snigger behind my hand. 'What a blessing he didn't come to our wedding!'

And there was me thinking mine were the only dysfunctional bowels around here!

'I shit you not!' he chuckles, marvelling at his clever pun. 'Come to think of it, that might be what Auntie Shirley was smelling earlier!'

'Eww, Christ. Why on earth was he invited tonight?' I ask, puzzled.

'Because he'd promised to be on his best behaviour.' Dan shrugs, eyes wandering back toward Uncle Tony who is busy seizing a scowling Crabby Gran by the shoulders.

'Come onnn, 'ave a dwink with me yer miserable old c—"

Hm, actually, I think I could grow to rather like Uncle Tony!

'Ye've hud enough tae sink a battleship, Tony! Git yer hands aff me. I'm away tae ma bed,' she hisses, storming off while a visibly seething Sharon shoots Rob a scathing look.

'I'm calling it now! I'm calling it now!' he attempts to pacify her, fumbling in his pocket for his phone.

Suddenly, Uncle Tony collapses onto the kitchen floor in a heap with a great slap, prompting all heads to turn.

'Quick! Get 'im outside for some air. I'll do him some strong coffee!' Auntie Shirley yells, darting toward the kettle just as the back door opens. Milliseconds later, Norbert bounds in, mounts Uncle Tony and starts humping him erratically while we all look on, open-mouthed. Mine and Dan's spontaneous bonk begins to pale in significance to Uncle Tony's antics and a reassured smile begins creeping up my face ... only to drop completely around three seconds later in a lightbulb moment.

'Ah, shit!' I gulp, clutching my face in horror.

'What? What is it?' Dan asks, looking worried.

'I think Mother's invited Uncle Tony to the christening!'

Chapter 6:

Take Me to Church

'**N**ow, I've told you before, dog. I don't care *how* well-connected you are, LEAVE THE POST ALONE!'

'Mother? Are you even listening to me?' I mutter down the line first thing next morning.

'Yes, yes. Sorry, dear. Have I sent out a christening invitation to whom?' she trills.

'Anthony Elliott!' I hiss urgently, head pounding.

'Ah, yes. Daniel's uncle. The one who drives around in that great big expensive car!' she sings, excitedly.

Wow. Is there anybody Mother doesn't know?

'Well, yes, but—'

'Yes, dear. His invite went out in yesterday's post. First class!' she boasts proudly.

Oh, fuck! Fuck! FUUUCK!

'Well, can you call Royal Mail and ask them not to deliver it?' I blurt in a panic.

'Whatever for?!'

'Well, he shouldn't really have been invited, Mother.'

'Of course, he should! He's family, isn't he?!'

'Yes but you need to uninvite him. Please, Mother, for the love of God, uninvite him!' I wail.

'Good grief! Why should I uninvite him, dear? Has he gone and killed somebody?'

'No, he's a p…' I begin, pausing to find a better way of putting it. 'He's a bit too fond of the booze!'

Mother lets out a silly little laugh in response. 'Goodness, dear. I think we've all been a little guilty of *that* at one point or another, nobody more so than yourself!'

'N-no, you don't understand. He's got a real problem!'

'Now, listen, dear. Hardworking men *need* to cut loose once in a while,' she excuses, irrespective of the fact that she doesn't know Uncle Tony from Adam and is purely basing her assessment of him as a "hardworking man" on the fact he drives a black Range Rover Sport on the rare occasions that he isn't pissed.

'Yes, but *he* cuts loose daily!' I plead.

'Well, perhaps he's just lonely? These executive types usually are. Goodness, I imagine it's all work and no play for the poor man!'

'Er, it's more the other way around actually, Moth—'

'Now, you needn't worry dear. I've a discerning eye for sifting out riff-raff!'

Hm, clearly not!

'And besides, I can't just go around uninviting people from guest lists. It's simply not the done thing!' she adds.

'But, Mother, I really think—'

'Now I must go, dear. Daddy and I are having afternoon tea with Councillor Shelbrooke, and that dog needs a firm hand!' she yells over me.

The line goes dead.

'She hung up on me!' I gasp in Dan's direction as he comes in from the bathroom.

'Well? Has she invited him or not?' he asks in nervous anticipation.

'*Yes*, she's invited him!' I reply through clenched teeth. 'She likes his car!'

'What?' Dan sneers in disbelief.

Suffice to say, if he drove a clapped-out Mondeo he'd be off the guestlist like a fucking shot!

'She spent most of the conversation making

excuses for him because she assumes he's well-to-do!'

'But Uncle Tony's *not* well-to-do, he's the bloody opposite!' Dan points out.

'Well, *we* know that but *she* doesn't, and there's no bloody telling her once her mind's made up!' I sigh defeatedly.

'Look at *you*, have you swallowed the sun or something?!' Becca grins up at me as I bluster out of the rain into Little Owlets on Monday morning.

'Eh? I thought I looked like shit?'

'Well, you do. We *all* do,' Becca replies unapologetically, peering around the room at the fellow mums among us, all sporting Fester Adams-like dark circles. 'But you've got that glow,' she adds. 'You know, the one you get when you've had a damn good seeing-to!'

I smirk guiltily.

'*Someone's* had a wild weekend!'

'Well, I guess you could call it that!' I half-smile, recalling the most embarrassing moment of my life thus far.

'Ha! Told you spontaneous sex was the best!'

Been there, done that, and moved onto risky public sex in one fell swoop, mate!

With neither the time, energy, nor gall to

reveal how experiencing our first shag in months was ruined by the nephew from hell, I simply nod in agreement, forcing a smile.

'Listen, Becca. I need your advice,' I tell her urgently, settling myself into a chair and rocking Jack's car seat with my foot.

'Look, if you're worried about the queefing, just see a quack, chick.'

Ugh! I've got to stop telling people too much!

I gulp, flushing pink. 'No, no. It's nothing to do with that. I need to find an excuse to uninvite somebody from the twins' christening.'

She chuckles wryly. 'Well, you can't uninvite the mother-in-law, unfortunately. Tried that one meself, many a time.'

'No, it's Dan's uncle. He's a pisshead,' I mouth at her.

'Aren't we all!'

Ugh, not her as well!

'No, what I mean is, he's got issues. You know, gets mouthy. Smashes stuff. Soils himself and that.'

'Is he a mate of my Jim's?' she says with a laugh.

'Ugh, I doubt it!' I groan. 'Look, he was a bloody embarrassment at my father-in-law's six-tieth at the weekend,' I go on, glancing sideward shadily on recalling that I wasn't all that conservative myself. 'The thing is, the reception is at my parents' place, and Mother is the worst snob! She'll do her nut if he so much as brushes against one of her ornaments.'

'Well, why in the hell did you invite the bloke knowing he's a piss-tank?' Becca frowns in dismay.

'I didn't! Mother did. She thinks he's some sort of rich, older playboy.'

'Well, just tell her he isn't and to uninvite him, then!'

'I've tried! She won't listen. Says it's not the done thing to go around uninviting people,' I groan.

Becca puffs out a deep and dubious exhalation of breath. 'Well, then, I can't think how you're going to get out of this one.' She frowns, biting her lip. 'I reckon some ornaments are about to get fucked up!'

'These christening gowns are bloody daft!' Dan scoffs, forcing Jack's over his head on the morning of the christening three weeks on. 'They look like curtains,' he goes on. 'Very *old* curtains!'

'They're the sort of thing royal babies wear for their christenings,' I reply, twirling the last section of hair around my waving wand. 'I think Mother's going for the royal touch.'

'Really?' Dan mutters, standing back from the bed in assessment. 'Looks more like the Oxfam touch to me.'

'I know, but it would've been more hassle than it was worth fighting her on it,' I mumble, reaching across to unplug the waving wand. 'It really affects my inner poise.'

'Right, well the twins are ready to rock and roll. Are you nearly done, babe? Your mum said we need to be at the church by 11.15am latest.'

'Now then, I *did* unplug the waver, I *did* unplug the waver, I *did* unplug the waver,' I chant, staring into space.

Dan frowns. 'Inner poise, you say?'

Arriving at the church and spying the large congregation outside it, any former poise quickly plummets in tandem with the autumn leaves descending the trees and line dancing across the road in the chilly wind.

'Where am I going to park?' Dan groans, crawling past the church in search of an ample space to leave the car.

'Anywhere far away enough for Mother not

to hear that exhaust!' I warn.

'Oh? Why's that?'

'Because this is a holy place of worship, not Silverstone,' I reply in a plummy voice.

Dan rolls his eyes, pulling onto a grassy verge.

'Well, I don't see Uncle Tony's Range Rover anywhere, do you reckon that means he's not coming after all?' I ask hopefully.

'No. I reckon it means he's left the car at home so he can get hammered,' Dan says with a laugh, sending a tsunami of anxiety crashing over me.

'Oh, God! Don't!' I gasp, bashing him playfully on the arm. 'And please tell me your dad had a quiet word in his ear like he promised!'

Dan shrugs, switching off the ignition. 'Well, he said he had when I spoke to him yesterday.'

'Still, it doesn't bring me much comfort. Not when I remember how effective his last "quiet word" was!' I fret, undoing my seatbelt while dangerous visions of Uncle Tony collapsed in a heap on the kitchen floor being humped by a Great Dane encircle my mind.

'Look, I'm sure it'll be okay. Christenings are usually pretty boring and formal. Uncle Tony only wants to be where the action is,' Dan reassures. 'He won't hang about. He'll probably just come to the service then get straight off to the pub!'

'You think?'

'Yeah. Honestly. I mean, he might not even turn up at all. He would've had a heavy night last night. Always does at the weekends. Try to relax. I don't think we've got anything to worry about.' He smiles, patting my knee.

'I thought you said that Mother told you we were all to arrive by 11.15 am latest,' I quiz Dan out on the church steps, juggling the babies between us. 'It's 11.21 am and she's not even here herself!' I add, scanning through the throngs of guests congregated among us in surprise.

And nor is Uncle Tony, I'm pleased to see!

'Yeah, she definitely said 11.15 am latest,' Dan shrugs.

'Oh, I get it! She'll be wanting to arrive last so everyone sees her.' I tut, shaking my head.

'Watcha, me old muckers!' comes Uncle Tony's voice over the din of the turnout. Heart sinking, I glance to my side to observe him climbing the church steps with a huge grin plastered on his face.

Let's hope that's the only thing to be plastered today!

I crane my neck to see if he's walking in a straight line or not, but I can't really tell.

'Over here, Tone!' Rob calls out from behind us.

'Now, *you* just remember our little chat earlier,' Sharon warns him behind me.

'Look, I've told you, it's sorted. He'll be good as gold,' Rob groans.

'Hold up! The bloody Queen's awwived,' Uncle Tony cackles, nodding behind him toward Dad's silver BMW drawing up at the bottom of the church steps.

Everyone stops and turns to look in silent anticipation as a dapper-looking Dad exits the driver's side and walks around to the near-side of the car. He opens the passenger door and Mother daintily holds out a white-gloved hand, twisting her legs elegantly to the side before rising to her feet and exiting the car in an extravagant ivory two-piece and what is easily the most ridiculous, fuck-off great hat yet!

'How long do you reckon they practised that?' Dan chuckles discreetly in my ear.

A series of disbelieving gasps follow as she gives us all a queenly wave and, with a satisfied smirk, takes Dad's arm and slowly begins climbing the church steps.

'Watcha, moosh!' Uncle Tony winks in her

direction. 'Look at *you* all done up like a dog's fackin' dinner!'

I can almost hear the national anthem screeching to a dramatic halt in my mind as she shoots him a look that would kill ten times over.

'Ooh, isn't it cold?' she laughs in a plummy voice, side-stepping Uncle Tony and making a beeline for me. 'Who invited that riff-raff?!' she demands through clenched teeth.

'*You* did!' I shrug back at her, adjusting Mia's shawl.

'Well, who on earth is he?'

'Dan's Uncle Tony. You know, he who drives around in that great big expensive car,' I remind her with glee.

'Well, I don't care for his manner.' She twitches, feathers shaking furiously on her hat. 'It's only 11.25 am and the man reeks to high heaven of whisky! I could smell it on the way past!'

'Well, I did try to warn you, Mother, but you were having none of it, remember?'

'Then you weren't persuasive enough!' she retorts, accusingly.

Oh, it's my fault! How didn't I guess?

'What time's kick off then?' Uncle Tony grins, marching toward us and rubbing his hands together.

'Somebody tell this fool he's at a christening and not a football match,' Mother groans mutedly in my direction.

A frosty silence ensues until Dad coughs awkwardly. 'Er, in a few minutes, I think,' he says, going on to make polite chit-chat while Mother grabs me by the arm and pulls me to the side.

'I will not have that man in my house after the service!' she fumes. 'Tell your in-laws to leave him outside.'

'He's not a dog!' I half-laugh.

'I don't care what he is. His name might be down but he's *not* coming in!'

'Calm down, Mother. Dan's not so sure he'll even come to the reception and if he does, he won't hang around. He'll be itching to get down the pub.'

She pauses, her beady eyes darting this way and that.

'Please, Mother, don't go kicking up a stink. This really isn't the time or place,' I plead.

'COOEY! COUNCILLOR SHELBROOKE, COOOEY!' she roars suddenly, waving manically and patting down her hat.

'Did you even hear any of that, Mother?' I scowl.

She emits a relenting sigh. 'Now listen to me, if he does show up then he is *not* to be given a drop of alcohol, you hear? Not a drop!' she barks. 'Hmph! That should get the desperado awf to the pub all the quicker!'

'And how am *I* supposed to see that he doesn't touch a drop of alcohol in between double feeds and nappy changes?' I huff, nodding down toward Mia lying in my arms.

'Well, I'm sure that between you and the Elliotts you'll manage it ... there's enough of you!' She frowns, peering down her nose at them all.

I nod, relentingly.

'And he's *not* to smoke those ghastly roll-ups in our garden, either!' she adds, thumbing toward Uncle Tony who is stood chatting next to Dad in a cloud of smoke.

I give another relenting nod.

'And there is to be *no* vulgar language,' she goes on. 'And that goes for you too, dear!'

I nod for the third time, rolling my eyes wearily.

'He is to sit down, quietly enjoy himself and keep the cockney slang to a minimum,' she concludes.

Hm. Not too sure Uncle Tony knows how to quietly enjoy himself, nor that it's a wise idea he sits down!

'Shall I ask him not to breathe?' I scoff.

'Now, don't be silly, dear!' she rebukes. 'Although it *would* keep the stench of whisky at bay.'

'Anything else?' I sigh, exasperated as Mia begins to wriggle in my arms.

'Yes! We're going to have to do something about that tie of his!' she fumes. 'Fancy turning up at the house of God with a wonky tie!'

Well, at least his flies are done up, I think to myself, though for how long is anyone's guess!

'Desmond! Pssst! Desmond!' Mother calls not-so-discreetly, flapping her hand to get his attention.

'Yes?' he asks with raised brows, strolling over toward us.

'Fix that man's tie!'

'I beg your pardon?'

'Fix his tie!' she groans. 'It's all wonky!'

'How on earth can I fix his tie? I can't just walk up and start manhandling him! I don't even know the man!' Dad protests.

'Then what better way to *get* to know him!' Mother fumes through clenched teeth. 'AH. Hello, Reverend!'

'She's off her head!' Dad gasps wide-eyed as Mother disappears from our sides. '*Completely* off her head!'

'Ah, looks like we're heading in,' Dan announces, waving everyone toward the church door where I spy Mother's mammoth hat disappearing in alongside Reverend Michaels.

'Could we all gather around the font, please,' the reverend announces over Mother's pretentious jibber-jabber. 'Yes, Mrs Bradshaw, I do only have the one hour in which to get this service done. There's another christening afterwards,' he mutters through an anaemic smile.

Jesus, even God's disciples get pissed off with her, I think to myself, nestling alongside our godparents – Dan's brother, Matt, chosen by Dan, and Councillor Shelbrooke, chosen by Mother.

The service begins with the hymn "Give Me Joy in My Heart", again chosen by Mother who seizes the opportunity to showcase her singing voice by projecting it loudly over the top of everyone else, giving us the opposite of joy in our hearts. I scan the pained-looking congregation and will it to be over quickly.

As Reverend Michaels goes on to deliver a long, monotonous passage from the Bible, I, by chance, look up just in time to catch Uncle Tony swigging from what looks like a hip flask hidden in his trouser pocket. Blood running cold, I nudge Dan and attempt to warn him with a series of panicked, coded facial expressions. He looks at me gone out, not guessing for a second that any of them meant 'Quick! Uncle Tony's on the lash already!'

'When's 'e gonna pass the wine and those bwead fings around, then?' Uncle Tony whispers loud enough to wake the dead buried out in the church grounds.

'They dinnay de that at christenings, Tony,' Crabby Gran enlightens him.

'Oh, weally? Bugger, I was looking forward to that!'

'Sssssssssh!' Mother hisses in disgust in their direction as Matt and Councillor Shelbrooke go on to make their declarations as godparents.

'Now then, if you'd like to hand me the firstborn,' Reverend Michael prompts, holding his arms out in readiness to baptise Jack over the font. 'I baptise Jack Aiden in the name of the Father, the Son and the Holy Spirit. Amen,' Reverend Michaels declares in a religious, robotic tone.

'Amen,' we repeat after him collectively as he hands Jack back to Dan. 'And now for the secondborn,' he prompts.

Aware that all eyes are on me, I hand Mia over carefully, batting away dangerous visions of myself clumsily dropping her in the font. My relief at having managed it faultlessly soon turns to horror as the loudest fart I've ever heard erupts from her and reverberates around the church for what seems like forever.

'Goodness, that wasn't very holy!' Reverend Michaels quips, prompting rounds of inflated laughter.

I glance toward Mother – the only one among us not laughing – stood under that ridiculous hat pursing her lips like a vexed giraffe.

'I baptise Mia Rose in the name of the Father, the Son and the Holy Spirit, amen,' Reverend Michaels declares. He marks the sign of the cross upon her forehead and then jokingly darts backward in horror, holding out the cross on the pendant he's wearing to repel the demon within her responsible for such ungodly wind, again prompting rounds of exaggerated laughter.

'Amen to that! Wight, let's go and wet the babies' 'eads!' Uncle Tony's voice booms around the church.

I've never been what I would call religious, but at that moment I find myself saying a little prayer to the man upstairs.

Chapter 7:

Brahms and Liszt

'I really think I ought to warn Mother about Uncle Tony's bowels,' I sigh, peering down at the beige patterned Chesterfield suite in dread as the clock runs down to his rumbustious arrival.

'I think she's got bigger problems by the look of it,' Dan remarks, nodding toward the dining area where Horatio is stood on top of the buffet table filling his boots.

'Quickly!' I gasp in part horror, part amusement. 'Get him down! She'll do her nu—'

An electrifying scream comes from inside the kitchen doorway.

Too late!

'Get that animal awf the table, Desmond! Quick! Quiiiiiick! The guests are arriving!' Mother screeches, head wobbling in outrage.

'Now come on, old boy, you can't be up here!' Dad reprimands him coolly, grabbing his collar before entering into a comical tug of war to get him off the table.

'Oh, for goodness sake, Desmond, show him who's boss!' Mother frowns, hands-on-hips.

'Well, that'd be *you*, my sweet,' Dad reminds her in a strained voice, writhing about and going red in the face in a battle the dog is clearly winning.

'My miniature toad in the holes!' Mother yells, clasping a hand to her mouth in horror as Horatio's face swings round to her.

'Can't you do anything with them?' Dad grunts.

'Of course I can't! They're beyond salvation! He's had all the toad and left us with the ruddy hole!' Mother cries.

Dad makes an addled expression before, in a sudden burst of strength – and impatience – he grabs Horatio around the middle and hoists him forcefully off the table.

Mother frantically sets about arranging the dilapidated buffet, jumping out of her skin at the loud and abrupt Big Ben-like chime of the doorbell. 'Answer the door would you, Desmond!' she yells, hurrying over to the dated sound system and hitting the play button triggering a chaotic explosion of Mozart's overture "Le Nozze De Figaro".

'Jesus, how are we meant to hear the baby

monitor?' Dan frowns, covering his ears.

I shrug nonchalantly, my mind consumed with far worse prospects as I glance out the front window to see streams of guests pooled upon the driveway, Uncle Tony and the Elliotts in amongst them. Gulping in horror and besieged with guilt, I dart off to warn Mother as Dad struggles to answer the door and restrain the dog simultaneously.

'Mother! Mother, listen. I really need to speak with you,' I yawp, skidding into the kitchen.

'Can't it wait, dear? I must see to the pea and mint croustades,' she heaves, rifling through the kitchen draw for a spoon.

'No, it can't! Well, not if you value your three-piece suite.'

She freezes, turning to face me in dread. 'If that dog has … If *that* dog!' she fumes, clenching her teeth.

'N-no, not the dog. It's Uncle Tony!'

She makes a contemptuous expression.

'He sometimes sh—er, fouls himself when he's had a drink,' I reveal, biting my lip. 'N-not all the time, just sometimes,' I add in a failed attempt to soften the blow.

'Then see to it that he *doesn't* have a drink!' she hisses.

'It's too late, he's been at it already! I saw him

with a hip flask in church.'

Mother freezes, dropping the spoon with a metallic clang. 'QUICK! Don't let him sit down!' she yells, hurtling off toward the front room at speed, me hot on her tail.

'—that's vewy civil of yer, I'll 'ave a bwandy and Coke if yer please, guv!' comes the tail-end of Uncle Tony's gruff, cockney twang from the front room.

Mother bursts in through the door just as he's about to sit down. 'Don't sit there!' she roars, making him jump.

He stops mid-air and slowly straightens up, turning to face her. 'Why? Is it reserved or summink?' He chuckles.

She freezes, her face twitching uncontrollably while the Elliotts exchange awkward glances.

'Alwight. Well, I'll sit 'ere then,' he mumbles, moving to sit in the armchair by the window.

'N-NO! Not there, either!' Mother booms, flapping her hand in angst. 'Or there,' she adds with an icy half-smile as he moves toward the adjacent sofa.

He rolls his eyes exasperatedly. 'Tell yer what, darlin', *you* tell me where you want me.'

'Well, couldn't you stand? Or *levitate*, perhaps?' she suggests, frowning down at his clodhopper shoes with a tut.

'He's nay a magician!' Crabby Gran scoffs, shaking her head.

Dan and I glance at one another in angst.

'It's probably going to be best if you stand, Tone,' Rob suggests, patting his shoulder.

'Er, where's yer shunkie, hen?' Gran pipes up.

Mother stares back at her. 'Pardon me?'

'Yer shunkie? Whereaboot is it?'

Mother's eyes dart toward me for clarity, but it's no good looking at me – I have a hard enough time understanding her myself!

'Er, Gran's asking to use the loo,' Dan quickly enlightens us all.

Mother laughs theatrically. 'Out in the hall on the right, dear. Goodness, don't the Scots have a strange vocabulary?' she chortles, patting down her hair pompously and missing the thunderous look Gran shoots her on her way out the door.

'Desmond, see to it that that man is offered mineral water and *only* mineral water!' Mother mutters firmly. 'And *do* stop that young boy from playing with my carriage clock. Now then, anyone for a fig surprise?' she trills, hurrying back off to the kitchen with no takers.

'Er, Toby, could you put the clock down please?' Dan asks him when neither Dad nor Lucie does.

'I need to get the batteries out of it first,' he replies matter-of-factly.

'*What?* What for?'

'For my robot.'

Dan pulls a face. 'But they're not yours, buddy. You can't just go around pinching other people's batteries.'

Yeah, yer liddle shit!

'Come on Toby, come with Nanny and we'll get you some lovely party food,' Sharon prompts in a sing-song voice, glittering off to the next room.

'Then can I have the batteries from that clock?' his whining voice trails off as he follows her through the open double-doors.

'And *I* had better get those drinks!' Dad smiles, making off for the kitchen. My eyes follow briefly as I wonder whether Uncle Tony will be getting that "bwandy and Coke" or, indeed, a glass of mineral water.

'Where's all the Party Rings and Oreos, Nanny?' Toby's disgruntled voice emanates from the dining room. 'This party food's crap—OUCH, Nanny! That hurt!'

An hour or so on and the place is bustling, a strange combination of plummy and thick cockney conversation ringing in the air. Much of it is centred around Matt and Laura's exotic breaks, but everything is seemingly civilised – save for Uncle Tony's erratic laugh, that is. Still, as long as he's only laughing and not fouling himself, then we're fine. In fact, with Toby busy leaf-picking for payment out in the back garden – Mother's unusually clever idea – I'd say everything's pretty hunky-dory! I glance down at my watch. If everything could only stay like this for just a couple more hours, we'll be laughing!

'I say, jolly good spread! Quite the culinary goddess, aren't we, sis?' Uncle Gerald chortles, half of it piled upon his plate, as Mother stands patting down her hair. 'Your Des seems to be enjoying himself,' he sniggers, nodding into the sitting room where Dad is frantically wrestling Horatio on the carpet to stop him jumping up on the sofas.

'Yes, well every rose has it's thorn,' she mutters distastefully, forcing plates of canapes under guests' noses, making them jump out their skins.

'Yes, well good food is good life, I say! Ruddy climate change is all they ever seem to talk about these days, don't you find?' he complains over a gob-full of pork pie at the buffet table behind me. 'Well, it's no good *me* going veggie! If I'm to live off Brussels sprouts for the rest of my days, then the greenhouse gases will go through the roof!'

His roar of laughter is cut short as he peers down toward his feet where Horatio is stood taking a leek up his trousers. 'DAHHHHHH!' he roars shaking his leg furiously as though it were on fire, commanding the full attention of the room.

'Oh, what are we going to do with you, Horatio?!' Mother scolds, wagging her finger at him.

Gerald scoffs. 'Well, if you ask me, you could start with a jolly good kick up the—'

'DESMOND! YOU'D BETTER LOAN POOR GERALD A CLEAN PAIR OF TROUSERS!'

'Yes, I'm only over here love, not in Australia!' Dad sighs, clutching his ears. 'Er, are you sure I'll have any to fit him,' he adds discreetly, peering across at Uncle Gerald's Santa-like physique.

'Just fetch him something elasticated!' Mother grunts through clenched teeth, grabbing Horatio firmly by his "genuine leather" dog collar and dragging him toward the back door.

Uncle Gerald peers around the room in embarrassment as everyone stands quietly gawping at his pissed corduroys. Then he turns to me. 'So! What went wrong between you and that American chap, old girl?' he booms, prompting me to instantly flush crimson. 'Was it because you went and piled all that weight back on?'

'Er, should we check on the twins?' Dan suggests, thumbing in the direction of the stairs while I slowly die inside.

'Hoy! Nay rumpy-pumpy this time!' Crabby

Gran warns, pointing a finger sternly at him.

'Rumpy-pumpy?' Uncle Gerald parrots, emitting a thunderous laugh.

'I'll come up and give you a hand, Danny. Lizzie, you stay here and enjoy yourself,' Sharon jumps in, heading off with Dan.

How embarrassing! What do they think we are, a couple of randy dogs they need to keep apart to stop them shagging every five seconds? Bugger me, that single, spontaneous bonk at Rob's sixtieth was more trouble than it was bloody worth!

'Didn't realise you were Scottish, old girl!' Uncle Gerald chuckles, looking Crabby Gran up and down under those great, unruly brows. 'I say, have you ever seen the Loch Ness monster?'

She pulls an expression akin to having just smelled a fart. 'Get aff! I'm away fae a ciggy!'

'*Right* little ray of sunshine, isn't she?' he laughs in her wake. 'Of course, it all goes back to William Wallace, you know. They won't let us forget, will they?'

Ouch!

Mortified, I glance apprehensively toward the rest of my in-laws, hoping to God all the merry talk of that "quickie in Cambodia" has been enough to distract them from Uncle Gerald's archaic, fat gob!

'You'd better pop upstairs and get changed,

Gerald. Here's a bag for your soiled trousers,' Mother interjects, breezing in at what is most opportune timing and thrusting a Marks and Sparks bag for life at him.

'Oh,' he mutters, face falling. 'Well, I'd better head up, then.'

'D'ya weckon we could 'ave some decent muuusic, moosh?' Uncle Tony slurs, creeping up behind Mother and grabbing her by the shoulders. 'This bloody Beethoven bollocks is doin' me nut in!'

'I'm afraid I don't care for your language!' she hisses in outrage, grasping both his hands and prising them from her shoulders. 'And furthermore, I would be grateful if you would stop referring to me by that ghastly name!'

'Alwwwight, I was only bein' fwiendly!' he mumbles, his glassy eyes following her across the room as she stomps off. 'She always this mardy?' he frowns.

'Yep!' I sigh.

'D'ya weckon she's got any Gunnns'n'Woses?' he slurs, checking out the sound system in the corner.

'I very much doubt it,' I mutter, stealing the opportunity to escape.

Two minutes on and Mother bursts into the conservatory demanding a word in my ear, just as I've sat down to eat.

'Elizabeth! There are people of substance here!' she fumes. 'I will *not* have that fool juggling with Scotch eggs in front of them!'

I frown, mouth full of cream cheese and chive puff, and crane my neck toward the dining room where I observe Uncle Tony doing just that. 'Knackers! Dwopped one!' he laughs as Councillor Shelbrooke watches on in astonishment.

'I've been angling tirelessly for a seat on the council committee,' Mother growls through clenched teeth, 'but it looks like that little dream is heading down the swanny as we speak!'

'Oh! So *that's* the real reason you insisted on *her* as Godmoth—'

Mother's maniacal shriek drowns me out and she earns herself some addled looks. She leans toward me, face contorted with rage. 'Now listen to me, I want that man out of here! Get rid of him! GET RID OF HIM!' she pants, prodding me.

'Alright, alright! I'll go and find Dan!' I sigh, rising out of my seat and walking off, exasperated, just as Dad plods toward me, ashen faced. 'You look like you've just seen a ghost!' I frown up at him.

'Well, I thought I was bloody well about to when the lock on the toilet door started turning all by itself,' he whimpers. 'Then the door flies open and that nephew of yours is stood there giggling and filming me on the toilet with his mother's phone!'

I peer back at him in astonishment, trying not to laugh. 'I've always said that kid's the devil child, but I didn't realise he had supernatural powers!'

'He hasn't! It was the old coin trick,' Dad fumes. 'Probably the fifty pence piece I'd paid him for leaf-picking earlier.'

'You only gave him a scabby fifty pence? That's child slave labour!' I laugh.

'Bloody generous if you ask me, considering the little tyke had barely covered a square foot before he downed tools,' Dad reveals in his defence. 'Do you think Dan might have a word and get the footage deleted before it ends up on that bloody TickyTok or whatever it's called?'

'Well, I was just off to speak to him about Uncle Tony; Mother wants him out,' I sigh with a weary head shake.

'Oh, that's going to have to wait, love. This is far more urgent. Tell you what, you go and find Dan and get that video deleted, I'll sort Uncle Tony.'

'Are you sure? You really think you can *sort* him?' I mutter dubiously, peering across the dining room in his direction to see him toss a glacé cherry in the air, attempt to catch it in his mouth and miss by miles. It sails through the air at speed, straight into Councillor Shelbrooke's handbag.

'Yes, leave it to me, love. I've been dealing with difficult people all my married life,' Dad insists, patting my shoulder. 'Hurry now, I've seen on the news how quickly these things can go viral!'

'Honestly, Dad. He's only six, he doesn't even know what social media...' I trail off, freezing as Toby walks past playing Candy Crush. 'Er, I'll get Dan, right away!'

∞∞∞

'He did *what*?!' Dan parrots back at me in shock up in the spare room.

'He burst in on Dad and filmed him on the toilet,' I repeat, flustered.

'How in the hell did he manage that?!'

'He opened the lock from the other side with a coin,' I sigh, absolutely sapped with it all. 'Lucie must've given him her phone to play with.'

'Well, you've got your Uncle Tony to thank for that one!' Sharon fumes. 'I warned him not to teach Toby stuff like that!'

Ah, of course. Who else could it have been?

Dan rolls his eyes and lets out a sluggish sigh, hurriedly fastening the poppers on Jack's romper suit.

'Ah, yes, and speak of the devil, Mother's

downstairs doing her nut. She wants him to leave,' I reveal awkwardly.

'Jesus, what's he done now?' Sharon gasps, sitting Mia up on her knee and fetching up her wind.

'I think so far it's mostly been limited to swearing and juggling with the buffet food, but it's probably wise to act now before we get into toilet territory,' I advise.

'And what the bloody hell's Rob doing while all this is going on?' she probes.

I shrug back at her, triggering a visible rise in her blood pressure.

'Here, you take Jack downstairs, babe,' Dan instructs, handing him over to me. 'I'll go find Lucie and get her to delete that bloody video off her phone. Oh, Mum, could you speak to Dad and arrange a cab for Uncle Tony?'

'Don't worry, I'm on it, son,' Sharon nods, the lack of sickening pet name for Dan a sign of her obviously fizzing anger.

We three – well, five if you count the babies – plough out of the spare room simultaneously to find Uncle Gerald stood on the landing, bursting out of an ancient pair of Dad's boldly-patterned eighties-style Bermuda shorts and clutching the bag for life containing his soiled trousers.

'If you ask me, that ruddy dog wants putting

down!' he seethes, moustache twitching. He turns and ambles off downstairs, leaving us all equally aghast. 'Oh, grow up! It was the fashion once,' his disgruntled tone reverberates back up the stairs as sniggers erupt from the hallway.

'ER...ERR, LET'S US LADIES HAVE COFFEE AND PETITS FOURS IN THE NEW CONSERVATORY!' Mother booms in an attempt to distract Councillor Shelbrooke from Uncle Gerald's unsightly cankles.

I'm sat bouncing Jack on my knee when Dan enters the living room some ten minutes later.

'Well, any joy?' I ask.

'The video's been deleted, and we think Uncle Tony already left. He's not in the house anywhere and nobody seems to know where he is,' he reveals.

I breathe a huge sigh of relief. 'Do you reckon he's gone down the pub?'

'More than likely.' He smiles.

'Thank God!' I gasp. My shoulders slump as the nervous tension leaves my body, only for it to make a swift return less than three seconds later when Mother storms in with her eyes out on stalks.

'Elizabeth! When I said I wanted that man out, I didn't mean out in the shed singing sea shanties with a bottle of your father's rum!' she hisses in my ear.

Ah.

'But Dad said he was going to sort it out,' I protest in my defence.

'Well, if your father's idea of "sorting it out" is taking him off to the shed and plying him with yet more alcohol, then *he's* part of the problem!' she seethes, hands-on-hips.

'You can hardly blame poor Dad—'

'Of course, I can. He's out there harmonising with the clown!'

Oh.

'Now get out there and tell your father to stop that carry on this instant!' she demands. 'I'm within a near inch of securing that seat on the committee, I can feel it in my bones!'

'Here, you take Jack,' I sigh, handing him over to Dan as Mother slinks off.

Venturing out through the back door, I'm met with a hubbub of shouting and laughter coming from the shed. I do a double-take as I venture down the path, looking across the garden to see Horatio digging up Mother's rose bush. Seeing that as the lesser of two evils, I rip open the shed door.

'Alwight, darlin? Pull up a bucket! We're 'avin' a bawwell of laughs out here!' Uncle Tony bellows with bloodshot eyes, his shirt unbuttoned to the waist and his tie wrapped around his forehead like a crap sort of makeshift Rambo bandana.

I glance at Dad beside him who looks much the same, only a lot less pissed. 'Er, what are you doing?'

'We're playing at being pirates, love.' He half-smiles.

'Ah. Could I have a word?'

He coughs, rising to his feet. We manoeuvre out of the shed and close the door on Uncle Tony belting out a solo, cockney rendition of "Soon May the Wellerman Come".

Hm. Looks like the Wellerman has already been... umpteen times over!

'What on earth are you doing, Dad? You were supposed to fix the problem, not add to it!' I demand, looking him up and down.

He shrugs. 'Well, it was the only way I could stop him crying, love.'

'Crying?' I parrot back at him in disbelief.

'Yes,' he mutters. 'That's the strange thing about the chap. He can be sobbing his heart out to you one minute, then trying to light his own wind the next!'

Good God!

'There's white spirit and all bloody sorts out

here. I've had a job trying to stop him drinking it, let alone stopping the place going up in flames!' he goes on.

'But why was *he* crying? It's the rest of us who should be bloody well crying!' I scoff.

'Well, when I took him aside in the kitchen and asked him to leave, he started bawling his eyes out. Going on about how he's the black sheep of the family and everyone hates him. I felt sorry for the poor chap.'

'So, you thought you'd take him out here, give him a load more booze and make everyone hate him even more?!' I ask, wide-eyed.

'No, of course not! I wanted him out of the house sharpish before your mother overheard him,' Dad reasons, but it's hard for me to take him seriously with that tie still wrapped around head. 'The rum was simply bait and, er, I thought I might as well grab a glass or two myself,' he adds through a guilty hiccup.

Just as I quietly compute the logic behind Dad's, determining that Uncle Tony would've been better left sobbing in the kitchen vs singing his heart out in the shed where the whole street can hear him, Mother appears in the back doorway like a pissed off panda. Her eyes dart from Dad to Horatio, to the rosebush, then back to Dad.

'DESMOND! Dress yourself properly!' she barks, steaming with rage as he whips off his pirate bandana and moves swiftly to do up his shirt buttons. 'And why haven't you gotten rid of that fool?!' she demands, clutching her head in dismay as the racket continues from the shed.

'Well, it's a little trickier than I thought. It seems he's quite the emotional drunk!' Dad whimpers diffidently.

'I don't care how emotional he is, I want him OUT!' Mother squawks.

'Yes, yes. I'm trying, pumpkin. I'm just at a loss with anything else to try,' Dad frowns, scratching his head.

'Shove his head under the hosepipe and his backside in a taxi!' Mother hisses, slamming the back door.

'Look, I'll go and fetch Rob, just try to keep him quiet for God's sake,' I say with a sigh, venturing back off into the house while Dad steels himself to enter the shed again.

'Yes, well it was ever so expensive. Cost us an arm and a leg!' Mother's shrill emanates from the conservatory. 'And it's a right little suntrap!'

'Rob, can I have a wor—' I begin, just as a blood-curdling scream rings out, making everyone jump in fright. I turn in horror and peer through the doorway to the conservatory to observe Uncle Tony slumped cross-eyed with his face pressed up against the outside glass, taking a long slash up it.

∞∞∞

'Well, that's everyone gone ... almost,' Dad mutters, plodding sheepishly into the front room. Mother sits perched on the sofa, white as a sheet and clutching a brandy, still visibly traumatised at her beloved new conservatory being used as a urinal ... and possibly at the sight of Uncle Tony's todger.

'I've never been so humiliated in all my life,' she sighs contemplatively, staring into space, trance-like.

Dad and I exchange anxious glances.

'Right, that's the twins ready to go,' Dan calls out from partway down the stairs in the hallway. 'Er, did everyone get away okay?' he asks, carrying the car seats into the front room.

Dad nods toward him. 'Yes, son.'

'And Uncle Tony?'

'Er, outside. Face-down in the chrysanthemums.'

Chapter 8:

Gobzilla

'Who's she?' I probe, glancing curiously at an unfamiliar woman with a teal-streaked blonde crop parading about the community centre hall with her toddler son dangling from her in a cloth baby sling, his feet touching her shins.

'Sonia Wilcox,' Becca mumbles, pulling a face without even turning behind to check who I was referring to. 'Don't make eye contact or she'll come over!' she warns, purposefully keeping her head down.

'So what if she does?' I shrug indifferently.

'Well, at a guess I'd say you'll end up wanting to hit her within thirty seconds flat.' Becca frowns.

'She can't be that bad!' I laugh, not buying for a second that there's anyone on this planet worse than Mother.

Becca leans toward me, smirking knowingly. 'Take every "Karen" in the United Kingdom, multiply by ten and you're still nowhere close,' she whispers.

I frown in bewilderment, glancing up just as Sonia – and massive enshrouded child – arrive at our table.

'Hi there, I'm Sonia,' she beams, reaching out a hand.

Well, she seems nice enough to me!

I shake it warmly, smiling up at her. 'Lizzie. Hi.'

'No, it's Sonia. S-O-N-I-A,' she replies loudly, as though she were talking to a three-year-old.

Cancel that, she's a twat!

I half-smile awkwardly. 'No, I mean *I'm* Lizzie.'

Ignoring me, she forcibly pulls up a chair. 'This is Eagle,' she announces, proudly. My gaze flicks toward the poor sod, cocooned like a chrysalis in that daft baby sling. 'We're bonding,' she explains through an unhinged grin that suggests the wheel is spinning but the hamster's snuffed it.

'Sorry?'

'That's what the sling's for, we're bonding. I suggest you do the same with yours, it's paying dividends!'

Paying dividends? He's got to be at least three. It's a wonder she hasn't slipped an effing disc!

I nod, trying not to judge. 'Well, these are my little ones. Jack and Mia.' I smile, pointing down toward the baby gym they're kicking away merrily upon.

'They're teething!' she gasps, clasping her clavicle dramatically – well, as much as she can over her son's covered head.

'Sorry?'

'They're teething! Look at the colour of their cheeks!'

I frown, peering down at them. 'Hm, well I'm not too sure about that. They've always been rosy-cheeked.'

She reaches across the table and clasps both my hands in hers. 'A mother knows!' she insists, solemnly.

'I *am* their mother' I murmur back at her, glancing at Becca who is trying to keep a straight face.

Suddenly, Eagle starts whingeing and thrashing around in his stripey organic cotton straitjacket.

Hold up, looks like bonding time's over!

'Eagle, relax!' Sonia commands. 'Relax and tell Mummy what it is you need.'

It's all I can do not to reach across the table, grasp both her hands and tell her firmly that 'a mother knows'.

'Mummy doesn't respond to screaming!' she cautions in a sing-song voice, refusing to budge as, clearly beyond relaxation, Eagle starts kicking off big time.

'He'll give up in a second. Bear with! Bear with!' she assures us, head jerking violently in her chair as all eyes turn toward our table. 'Alright, alright. Get down then!' she shouts, forced into submission when, in living up to his bird of prey namesake, Eagle begins savagely clawing at her face.

Christ, looks like all that bonding's really paying dividends!

No sooner than that ridiculous sling is undone, he springs from her lap and makes a frantic dash for freedom.

'He's harbouring a load of negative energy,' she excuses, quickly rising from her seat. 'I think I'll do a chakra cleanse on him this evening.'

Why not just let the poor bugger walk, love?!

'Anyway, peace out,' she says with a wink, before turning around. 'Eaaaagle, snack time!' she yells, chasing him across the hall with mad eyes and a celery stick she's produced from her bag.

Peace off!

Becca and I look at one another in silence. Sometimes there are just no words!

∞∞∞

Struggling in out of the cold with the twins later that afternoon, a flashing from the answer machine catches my eye. Overloaded with coats, hats and mittens, I insouciantly hit the play button on my way over to the coat pegs, bracing myself for Mother's shrill.

'Dan, hi! This is Amber Ross,' comes a voice oozing confidence and sophistication.

I freeze in position, all ears.

'If you could give me a call back as soon as you get this, that'd be awesome. You've got my number, so catch up with you soon. Take care, byeee!'

'Okay, who's Amber Ross when she's at home?' I muse, clicking my tongue. Well, whoever she is, she sounds very fun and vogue. A total stranger to me, obviously, but that doesn't stop the fast-forming mental image I'm seeing of a tall, slim, supermodel from Planet Peng!

Inner Twat: *How dare Dan have supermodels calling our home!*

Later, while ramming a ready-made, heavily discounted shepherd's pie into the grimy oven, my thoughts are consumed with the mystery surrounding Dan's connection with this seemingly young and vivacious female…

Plausible explanations:

1: She's a fitness client of his.

2: It's about something he's planning for my birthday in a few weeks.

3: He's got a bit on the side!

Well, let's see now. Number one is perfectly probable. Dan still trains a select few people now and again at the weekends for some extra cash, although I can't pretend to be cool with him training someone with such a great name. Why can't she be a Julie? Julie's okay. I'd have been totally cool with a Julie! As for number two … yep, also perfectly probable. In fact, *love* the idea of number two! And number three? No. That's just ridiculous and I'm an idiot of the highest order for even entertaining the idea!

As Dan's key hits the lock just before 6pm – and with me sat on the sofa staring into space, *still* entertaining the idea of number three – I decide to take the direct approach…

'Do you have a secret girlfriend called Amber Ross?' I blurt before he's even an inch through the front door.

'Sorry?!'

'Erm, I mean, someone called Amber Ross called for you. She left a voicemail.'

'Oh, really?' he replies from the doorway, his face lighting up.

Inner twat: *There, see? Told you she's his mistress! Just look what the mere mention of her name does to him!*

'So, who is she?' I ask, cool but not cool.

'Well, you know that sales job I applied for with Pepped, the energy drinks company?'

'Uh-huh?'

'She's the sales manager there! So it's probably about my application!' he beams.

Inner twat: *Damn. All totally innocent. Life just got boring again!*

'The salary is almost double what I'm earning now! If I land this, we can get that mortgage, babe!' he goes on.

Suddenly, my mind is a conveyor belt of images of a three-bed new-build in the suburbs, all done out from top to bottom in contemporary grey and crisp white with a place for everything and everything in its place.

'Oh my God! Well, hadn't you better call her back then?' I suggest, beginning to lose my shit at the thought of candles, cosy throws, and co-ordinating karate-chopped scatter cushions.

'Yeah, I'll do it now,' he says, rushing over to the landline. 'Er, could you maybe turn the TV down first? I can't call her with all that oinking in the background.'

'Oh, sorry.' I reach forward to grab the remote to turn Peppa Pig down. 'They, er, seem to like the colours on the screen,' I excuse.

Dan gives me a pointed look, then gestures with the phone toward the twins who are sat in their bouncy chairs, eating their fists and looking everywhere but at the television.

Okay, so children's television seems to have opened up a whole new world of escapism for me. There, I said it.

'Hi Amber, it's Dan Elliott. You left a message earlier asking me to call?'

A pause follows and I brace myself, eyes fixated on him, hoping and praying that it's good news. Surely she wouldn't phone if it wasn't?

'Oh, wow! That's great news!' he beams, looking over at me and giving me the thumbs-up.

Yaaaaaas! Oh my God! Oh my God! Oh my God! I haven't been this excited since KFC opened a drive-thru in the next street but one! Everything's about to change for the better. Our own home! A fresh start! What better incentive is there to become a clean, neat and organised person? Ha! I'm going to be one of those people who refrigerates absolutely everything!

∞ ∞ ∞

A week on, with Dan's notice period served and having packed him off with all the hugs and good luck in the world for his first day in the new job, life has definitely taken an amazing turn. I've found our dream home – and am already mentally living there – circled half the Argos catalogue and am excitedly forfeiting my sleeping hours for entranced viewings of the gleaming, pristine homes of just about every home decor YouTuber. *Yes*, Dan may not have even set foot upon the premises of his new employer yet, but I'm looking to the future and, now more than ever, it's looking bright.

Well, at least it *was* until my phone started ringing.

Bugger, it's Mother. Do I answer and risk destroying this pleasurable new-found high? Oh, it's rung off. Good, I suppose? No, wait, it's ringing again. Well, perhaps I'd better answer, must be important…

'Hello?'

'Ah, thank goodness! There you are!'

Oh God, it sounds urgent. Please don't let Dad have had a breakdown! Please don't let Dad have had a breakdown!

'Auntie Val has just bought a wonderful little

place out on the French Riviera, dear!'

Oh.

'Good for her!' I remark, daring to hope that I might join Auntie Val on the property ladder at some point before I snuff it.

'Yes, isn't it? Some people have all the luck, and then there are the rest of us,' she complains. 'Well, I've been thinking and I've been trying to remember when the last time was that I was happy … I mean, *truly* happy.'

Yawn.

'And I h-hate to say it, but I can't r-remember,' she howls, bursting into tears on the other end of the line.

Great! Mother in self-pity mode. Just what I bloody need!

'Oh, Mother! Don't be daft. You? Unhappy? I mean, what in the world have you got to be unhappy about?'

'Well, I'm the l-laughing-stock at the c-country club and my friends have all disowned me since that d-disastrous christening,' she wails.

'It was hardly a disaster, Mother! A drunken man took a slash up your conservatory. Nobody died!' I argue. 'Besides, it was probably the most excitement those stuffy old bags have had in years!'

'Oh, you're just like your father! He never listens either!' she sobs.

'I'm listening, Mother. I just think you're being very silly!' I reply, ears throbbing from the cacophony. 'What's done is done and these things happen to the best of people. If your so-called friends are prepared to disown you over something so daft, then they're not friends.'

She goes quiet, other than for the occasional sniff. 'Well, anyway. I need a holiday! I need to get away from it all before I go stir-crazy,' she announces dramatically. 'Beach walks, fresh air, French cuisine! The French Riviera is the perfect panacea!'

'Well, what are you waiting for then? Get on the phone to Auntie Val and arrange something!' I prompt, rolling my eyes.

'Oh, I've done that, dear' she replies, suddenly remarkably composed. 'We've an open invitation so we thought it might be nice to get away before Christmas. The problem is Horatio. He doesn't like other dogs so I can't put him in the kennels. I think it's best for all concerned that *you* come and stay here at ours and dog-sit for a week.'

'Absolutely no way!' I nearly choke.

'But why, dear?'

Do I even need to answer that?

'Because I have a life, Mother! A husband and three-month-old twins, in case you hadn't noticed.'

'Well, bring them along!' she trills.

'No, Mother! We can't just uproot our lives and move into your place for a week,' I fume, still not entirely believing I'm having this conversation. 'Dan's just started his new job, we're ... well, *I'm* house-hunting and besides, who'd be looking after our place?'

She laughs mockingly. 'Good grief, dear. It's only a pokey little rented flat. Anyone would think it was a place on Sandbanks the way you go on!'

'Mother, I'm not having the dog, okay?!'

Wow, get me!

'Oh,' she sighs glumly. Then the waterworks start again. 'W-well, don't worry about me. I'll j-just fester away with no friends and n-nothing to look forward to,' she wails. 'I'll spend the last part of my life in mis—'

'Okay! Okay! How about you bring him here?' I offer before I've registered the words in my brain.

'Yes, dear. That could work!' she booms delightedly after a three-second pause. 'Right, I'm awf to book our flights!'

Oh fuck, what have I done?!

If it wasn't bad enough that I've just volunteered

to add a boisterous, out-of-control corgi to my long list of responsibilities, my day takes a dramatic nosedive when, during a mid-afternoon nose at Pepped Drinks Co's LinkedIn, I unwittingly discover that Dan's new boss is hot as hell! In fact, she's looks just like Margot Robbie, with shoulder-length hair of honey-blonde silk, doe-like bluey-green eyes, insanely good brows and everything perfectly proportioned and chiselled upon a canvas of smooth, doll-like skin. All the proof I need that God, if he exists, has favourites. Ugh! *And* she has a nose. *And* a jawline. *And* it doesn't look like she needs to give her camera lens a bloody good wipe! Damn, that means it's not just filters. This Margot lookalike smiling back at me with super-star teeth is the *real deal* and my husband – who goes especially quiet during certain scenes in *The Wolf of Wall Street* – is going to be around her eight and a half hours per day, five days a week. Holy flaps!

Inner voice of reason:

1. *Margot or not, this job is a blessing and nobody deserves it more than Dan.*

2. *Struggling up flights of stairs with a child in one arm and infant carrier in the other is soon to be a thing of the past!*

3. *No more scanning supermarket shelves for half price labels!*

4. *Long, romantic summer nights on the patio*

*of our new home with bowl of olives and bot-
tle of Prosecco.*

5. *Spontaneous al fresco sex (provided can lose
   four stone again and acquire overnight sexual prowess of porn star!).*

6. *Amber Ross is the reason for all of the above,
   she should be celebrated!*

Inner twat:

Staring in adulation at her polished, prepos-
sessing profile pic, I suddenly feel about as alluring
as Sloth from *The Goonies*. No, no, no! I absolutely,
categorically refuse to let my insecurities get the
better of me. Jealousy is a disease! I'm better than
that! Amber Ross chose my Dan over all the other
applicants for this job she could have picked, and
it's opened up a whole new world of possibility
for our family. I am grateful to Amber Ross, even
if the arrival of a Margot Robbie lookalike into my
husband's daily life couldn't have come at a worse
effing time!

Emergency Plan of action:

1. *Will lose fifty stone!*
2. *Will get easily manageable, sleek new hair-
   style in place of electric-shock look.*
3. *Will replace holey F&F at Tesco leggings
   and baggy, bobbly jumpers with sophisticated, co-ordinated outfits.*

4. *Will find array of sexy knickers that hide gut and arse, while leaving little to the imagination.*
5. *Will do daily pelvic floor exercises religiously so can be a tighter wife.*
6. *Will fall in love with cleaning, acquiring domestic excellence of Mrs Hinch!*
7. *Will fall in love with cooking, acquiring culinary excellence of Gordon Ramsay!*
8. *Will fall in love with parenting, acquiring poise and order of Nanny McPhee!*

Then, once all that's done, I'll go out and climb Mount Everest on one effing leg.

∞∞∞

'Well, how was your first day?!' I badger Dan as soon as he's home.

'Well, it was mostly training but wow! What a great place to work!' he enthuses, stepping inside and whipping off his jacket.

'Really?' I remark, eyes furiously scanning his face for the slightest clue that he's in love with her.

He grins from ear to ear. 'God, yeah! They treat their staff so well. Amber isn't like a manager, she's more like a mate. We're honestly like one big family!'

Okay, I might be able to handle that, so long as she doesn't loom naked in doorways wearing only black lace stockings and stilettos!

'Awww, great!' I gush with a bogus smile.

'Yeah! And they allow you free unlimited hot and cold drinks all day!' he goes on.

'Awesome!' I chirp enthusiastically.

'And they even have a massive tunnel slide in the main office. Honest! You can either enter via the slide or just use the door to get in.'

What the actual...?

'And they lay on free fruit!'

'Amazing!' I declare approvingly.

'And I get an hour for lunch and two fifteen-minute tea breaks!'

'Fantastic!' I cheer fervently.

'And Amber takes the team away every quarter for team-building weekends. You know, stuff like white water rafting, abseiling, go-karting, that sort of thing!' he concludes, instantly wiping the smile off my face while the macabre movie score from *Cape Fear* blasts out in my head at a thousand decibels.

My husband. Staying away in a hotel all weekend with his hot boss.

HOLY MOTHER OF FUCK!

Chapter 9:

Cake Wars

Occasion: **Dan's birthday**

Objective: **Blow his socks off with amazing meal and tantric sex!**

'Oh, God! Why does Jamie Oliver make it look so easy,' I bawl at my phone, closing down his Thai green curry FoodTube tutorial in disgust. I mean, he doesn't even measure out his ingredients, he just goes by chef's intuition. Great if you're Jamie, but not so great for a tit like me who needs everything spelled out to them. I mean, what constitutes a pinch? A drizzle? A good glug? Christ only knows! Cooking's like chlamydia: you've either got it or you haven't ... and I've never had it, on either count.

With Dan having accrued no annual leave in the new job as yet – Pepped Drinks Co's generously long list of employee benefits not quite stretching as far as "your birthday off" – and with my birthday and Christmas just around the corner, a cheap and cheerful evening celebration at home is looking like the only option for tomorrow. Still, Dan's never been one for a fuss and I know he'll appreciate anything I do for him.

With that, I bundle up and take myself and the twins off down the high street to spend the TV licence on birthday provisions. We only watch Peppa Pig these days, so what do we need a TV licence for anyway? They can cart me off to the nick all they like; I've always said I could benefit from some jail time for the restricted meals and forced exercise!

While out, I catch sight of myself in the shop window of Curry's, am duly appalled and decide I need a change. Something to perk me up. Something to give me a lift. But also something that can be done on the cheap...

Going blonde, obviously!

They do say blondes have more fun. Fun is good. *Yes* to fun. *Yes* to blonde!

Okay, most people visit the hairdresser over the course of several weeks to achieve a dramatically lighter colour result, but, as I wind my merry way into Boots to spend my Advantage Card points on box dyes, I get to feeling that, since there's nothing one cannot learn from YouTube, hairdressers are a bit of a non-necessity these days. Besides, the colour chart on the back of the box very clearly shows a golden blonde colour result next to my shade of brown. It's all in an afternoon's work!

∞ ∞ ∞

'Happy birthday, darling,' I greet Dan excitedly next morning, proud of the little birthday display I got up early to arrange.

He bursts into the front room, mumbling something about his car keys being missing and not even noticing the banners nor the balloons I almost passed out blowing up.

'Well? What do you think?' I nudge, hopefully.

'Sorry?' he murmurs, looking up for all of two seconds. 'Aww, that's lovely, but I'm so late!' He half-smiles, one eye in my direction and the other scouring every surface for his keys.

'You've got a few minutes to sit and open your cards and presents, surely?' I challenge.

He says nothing, hurriedly tearing open draws and turning over cushions.

'Dan, I can see them from here. They're on top of the TV,' I tell him, patting the sofa beside me as a gesture for him to sit down.

'Ah, phew! Cheers,' he pants, snatching them up. 'Look, I've really gotta go. Let's do this tonight, yeah?' He smiles, pecks me on the cheek and leaves me silently stunned on the sofa in my Betty Boop pyjamas.

Mental observations:

1: No lips, seriously?

2: Barely any acknowledgement of the effort I went to for him. Cheater's guilt, perhaps?

3: On reflection, it's a good job he didn't notice the birthday banners, which I've only just noticed say "Happy Retirement" instead of "Happy Birthday".

Inner voice of reason: *Alright, he was late this morning. He didn't notice the effort I put in. That's okay. He'll notice when he comes home. By which time I'll be blonde and will have all the ironing done that's been taking up the length and breadth of the kitchen table for nigh-on the last fortnight, with said table set for a birthday meal-for-two: creamy Tuscan chicken with seasonal veg, followed by raspberry and white chocolate cheesecake ... and tantric sex.*

Later, with the twins fed and babbling away contentedly in their bouncy chairs, I load up YouTube and browse the many offerings in dark-to-blonde home hair transformations. I sit and watch the first few minutes of the selected video, but it's not long before excitement takes over, said tutorial is duly abandoned, and Operation Blonde Bombshell is launched!

With the lightening process underway, my head bound and wrapped in clingfilm and a towel turban, I crack on tackling the Kilimanjaro of crumpled clothes lying in a heap on the kitchen table. Before too long I've steamed through the worst of it, singing and swaying along to the old school dance anthems on the radio, knowing that with every passing second I'm transforming!

Just as I'm finishing up the last of Dan's many work shirts, the radio presenter cuts in with an announcement. 'Gotta say a massive happy birthday to Dan Elliott, aka Mr Guns, from Ambs and all the team at Pepped. Enjoy the celebrations later on!'

Celebrations? What celebrations?!

I freeze, only coming to when the smell of burning arouses my senses, prompting me to glance down to see a perfect smoking brown imprint of the iron on Dan's white Hugo Boss shirt from way back when he could afford designer labels. Shit! But still, *Mr Guns?*! How very dare she?! *My* guns! *My* precious! Pfft! And she's scraping the barrel for pet names with "Ambs"! It's abbreviation for the hell of it. But still, pet name terms already?! This is worse than I'd thought.

A lava-like rage bubbles within me as my

thoughts go into overdrive.

Mental calculation:

Pet names = non-professional working environment.

Non-professional working environment = flirting.

Flirting + non-professional working environment = illicit sexual affair!

But really, though? Would Dan cheat on me? Would he do the dirty on his young family? Neurotic as I am, I'm still inclined to say no at this stage. Although, I'm so sure what Amber's position is … missionary, probably!

I spend the following few minutes singing along zealously to Brandy's "The Boy is Mine" while death-staring the fridge as though it were Amber, then opening it in search of non-existential interesting snacks.

Mind totally preoccupied with what else "Ambs" might have planned for my husband's birthday – as well as getting the twins down for their naps – I forget about the bleach currently burning away and doing it's thang on my nut … till the insane itching starts, at which point I catapult into the bathroom, flip my head over the bath and begin frantically rinsing it out, trying to reserve all judgement until it's fully dried.

'WHAT THE FFFFFF!' I gasp at the multicoloured neon hotchpotch reflected back at me in the mirror. The roots are fluorescent yellow, the ends are fiery red, I can't get a comb through the bastard, and it looks absolutely nothing like the grinning Paris Hilton lookalike on the front of the box!

Okay, deep breaths, Lizzie, deep breaths! We've still got the toner stage. The toner will totally fix this!

30 minutes later...

Okay, I'm grey. Not even a trendy grey – we're talking Pound Shop Halloween witch's wig grey!

Fuck. FUCK!

To think that the whole point of this process was to give my look a lift. Well, it's given it a lift alright. A lift to 2062! I no longer look frumpy, I look *old* and bloody frumpy! *And* I paid for the privilege in juicy Advantage Card points that I'll never get back. Gahhhhhh!

The only thing left to do is rubber stamp this entire experience a "complete and utter waste of time" and revert back to my original colour. Mousy brown is simple. Mousy brown is low maintenance. *Yes* to mousy brown! Gentlemen may very well prefer blondes, but I'm sure that when faced with a choice of mousy brown or evil peddler woman grey, it'd be mousy brown every time. At least that's the best possible way of looking at it.

Okay. Hair dye. We need more hair dye. But the twins are sleeping, so I can't leave the flat...

Only Deliveroo can save me now!

∞∞∞

'How was your day, birthday boy?' I grin as Dan walks in through the door that evening. I pat down my knackered ends and eye the curious posh looking drawcord bag he places down beside his feet.

'Hey, babe, it was great,' he smiles, walking over to greet me with a kiss on the lips.

'We've got you a cake!' I announce, clapping my hands with glee. 'Colin the Caterpillar, of course! No birthday's a birthday without Colin the Caterpillar.'

'Yeesh! *More* cake?' He groans, rubbing his belly as the elevated grin on my face disintegrates.

'What do you mean?'

'Amber and the team got me this,' he says, sliding out what looks to be a large bakery box from the posh looking drawcord bag. He opens it back to reveal a massive, expertly designed, partially sliced bicep cake, professionally iced with what is obviously her flirty nickname for him.

'"Happy Birthday, Mr Guns",' I read aloud.

Suddenly, Colin the Caterpillar looks like a pile of shite.

Great!

'As you can see, we were nowhere near finishing it, so I brought it home. Thought you could see off the rest of it.'

'Oh, charming,' I mutter, miffed at the idea that an entire sales team couldn't finish it, but clearly Dan thinks I can. I mean, I probably can, but totally not the point.

He frowns back at me. 'Sorry?'

'Well, I like cake, but God, Dan! You make me sound like Augustus Gloop!

'I didn't mean to offend you, babe. But you did eat three of the four tiers of our wedding cake, remember?' he says with a chuckle and a shrug.

'Well … well,' I stumble, cheeks reddening and face twitching. 'That was only because there was so much of it left and it was just going to go to waste.'

'Exactly. That's why I thought I'd bring this one home for you to finish off,' he reasons.

Voice in head: *Wow, he makes me sound like a professional eater. I'm sure I read somewhere that constant put-downs from your other half is a sign that they're cheating. We're only on put-down number one so far, but yeah. You know what? I wouldn't dream of eating this effing great cake out of principal!*

I mean, every pound gained from the bastard would be Amber Ross's doing. It's as good as willingly drinking the enemy's poison.

'Well? Do you want the bloody thing or not?' Dan asks in an elevated voice that tells me if I don't let this go then tonight's birthday tea may very well end with some cake-throwing.

'Okay, put it in the kitchen,' I relent in a low tone, making a mental note to avoid it like the plague and let it go stale, just to prove to him that I can take cake or leave it. I'll probably end up taking it to be fair, but yeah.

'I've made you a lovely dinner,' I announce, remembering my culinary masterpiece and heading into the kitchen to check on its progress. 'Should be just about done.'

They do say the way to a man's heart is through his stomach, I think to myself as I forage through the kitchen drawer for the oven glove. Well, let's put that sentiment to the test, shall we? Yanking open the oven door, I stare in disbelief at my uncooked and stone-cold culinary masterpiece.

Fuck! Forgot to set the temperature.

Have I got time for a quick shower before you dish up?' he calls after me.

'Er, yeah! Go have your shower, Dan,' I call out over my shoulder.

Heck, have ten!

∞ ∞ ∞

Half an hour or so later…

'Wow. Looks amazing,' he gushes, lowering into his chair at the table and hungrily eyeing his plate. 'Hey, where did all that ironing go? Did you shove it in a cupboard?'

Ding! Second put-down this evening.

'I did it all this afternoon,' I reveal, plodding over to join him.

I also went from brown to orange to grey and back, but I'm not about to tell him that.

'Oh, really? Wow!' he exclaims, looking around. 'And the place is gleaming too I notice.'

Well, on the surface at least.

'Proper domestic goddess,' he remarks.

Mental note: *Ah, a compliment! But is it, though? It's hardly an honour being told you made a good job of the cleaning.*

I smile coyly, reaching for the wine as he moves to tuck into my culinary triumph.

'Cooked with love,' I nod toward him, proudly.

'Hm.' He frowns, examining it closely. 'Chicken's still pink in the middle.'

Okay, cooked irresponsibly then!

'Isn't all chicken a little bit pink, though?' I excuse over a fake laugh, lunging for my wine glass and necking it back.

'No, it has to be cooked through. Raw chicken's lethal,' he says in a serious tone. 'If this were any pinker, it'd be clucking, babe!' He chuckles, pushing his plate away.

My creamy Tuscan chicken! My beautiful but undercooked creamy Tuscan chicken! Spurned. Rebuffed. Rejected. What the cluck?!

'But it shouldn't be undercooked! I turned the oven temperature right up so that it would cook quicker. I thought it was burning. It's had a proper blasting,' I protest, wide-eyed.

'Well, that's no good. All that does is burn the outside and leave the inside raw,' he reasons, taking out his phone from his pocket as it pings with a text.

Voice in head: *It's her! She can't leave him alone! She's been with him for most of the day and still she can't leave him alone!*

'Who's that?' I ask in a fraudulently casual tone.

'Just more birthday wishes,' he mumbles.

Hm.

'Well, um, I could pop the food back into the

oven for a bit?' I offer feebly.

'No, it's okay, honestly. I wasn't that hungry to begin with,' he mutters, tapping away.

'Well … well, let's get straight onto dessert then, shall we?' I pant, keen to end things on a sweet note. Everyone knows dessert is the best part of a meal, anyway. I would've happily skipped dinner and plunged straight into dessert as a child. Dan may be a grown arse adult in need of a sufficient meal after being at work all day, but still.

'Ooh! What've we got?' he asks.

'Raspberry and white chocolate cheesecake!' I announce with glee, getting up to retrieve it from the kitchen.

'Nice!' he exclaims, back to tapping away on his phone with a preoccupied smile.

'Here we go, tuck in!' I chirp, placing a bowl down in front of him and hovering briefly as he places his phone down on the table beside him. And then I see it … a WhatsApp message pop-up on the screen from Amber! What the hell?! He said it was just more birthday wishes. She's already called into the radio station *and* organised him a fuck-off great birthday cake. How many more birthday wishes does this woman need to send to a married father-of-two on her team at work?!

'Something the matter?' Dan asks as I stand with squinted eyes, trying desperately to read it upside down.

'Er … no,' I mutter, sitting down reluctantly.

He picks up his spoon and breaks into his cheesecake … with great difficulty it would appear. For God's sake, *now* what's bloody wrong?!

'What's up?' I ask with a frown.

'It's frozen,' he replies, prodding it about the bowl.

'Well, it was a bit cheaper than buying chilled,' I excuse, trying – and failing – to break into my own.

'I mean it's frozen solid,' he reiterates. 'You *do* know you have to defrost frozen cheesecake?'

'Eh?'

'The cheesecake. You defrosted it, right?'

I shrug. 'No? It's a frozen dessert, isn't it? Like ice cream.'

He gives me a look that signals tantric birthday sex may be compromised. 'Er, no. Frozen cheesecake needs to be defrosted,' he mutters, placing down his spoon with a chink.

Bam! There goes my Dan Elliott award for domestic goddessery.

'Right,' I mumble, glowing pink.

Inner Voice of Reason: *Jesus, Lizzie! Here you are, up against Margot Robbie's body double with her* *effing great cake, and you're serving him up raw and frozen food!*

'Where are you going?' I ask, as he rises up out of his chair.

Inner twat: *He's leaving you for Margot.*

'Thought I'd open my presents, babe,' he says, wandering over toward the birthday display still neatly arranged on the coffee table from this morning.

Good! At least none of them are raw or frozen.

He smiles as he unwraps a funky tie, socks, Lynx Duo and £25 Amazon gift card. 'Thanks, babe.'

'Did they get you a present at work?' I ask, not thinking for a moment that they did. I mean, the cake alone must've cost an arm and a leg. Dan's just a newbie – he was lucky just to get even that.

'Yeah, an Amazon gift card,' he reveals, brandishing it from his pocket.

Wow. Pied by Margot for the second time today.

'Oh,' I mutter, 'how much?'

'Fifty quid.'

And that's a hat-trick!

'I can put yours to it to get something,' he says, making it sound as second-best as I feel right now.

Suddenly, unable to contain it any longer, I let out a strange sort of pent-up wail.

He looks at me gone out. 'Er ... what was that?'

'It's just ... just ... well, you could at least pretend to be a bit more grateful, Dan. I went to a lot of trouble to do this for you tonight and it seems to me that you've had a whale of a time at work today and couldn't care less about your birthday tea.'

'Well, you did nearly give me the gift of salmonella, babe.' He chuckles, face crumpling when he sees I'm not laughing.

'Oh, stop being dramatic! Nobody got salmonella,' I hiss.

'Only because I was vigilant enough to see it wasn't cooked properly,' he points out.

Ooosh! Undercooked chicken or not, I'm still counting that one as the third put-down of the evening.

'Well ... well, I haven't seen you all day and all I've had is half-smiles and shrugs out of you,' I retort, folding my arms defensively.

'Well, what do you want me to do? How do you want me to act?' he challenges, shaking his head.

A crying fit erupts from the bedroom.

'Right, that's it, I've had it!' I bawl.

'It's okay, I'll go. Er, where are you going?' he quizzes me, looking concerned as I storm to the front door, yank my coat from the peg and pull it on viciously.

'I'm going out to buy dummies, Dan. And don't even try to stop me!' I reply through clenched teeth as though I were committing the worst sin in the world. 'I mean it! I'm through with trying to do everything by the book. I'm only human. There's only so much I can take.'

'Okay, okay!' he gasps, 'but—'

'But nothing!' I explode.

'No, honestly, Lizzie—'

'WHAT?!'

'You might want to do your flies up first.'

Oh.

Chapter 10:

Date Night

Dan: *Going to be late tonight babe, not sure when I'll be home. Don't worry about tea, I'll grab something while I'm out. D x*

OMG, and so it begins already! The coming home late, the distant texts; yeesh!

Me: *Don't they have to give you notice if they want you to work late? Do you really have to stay behind? Miss you! :-(x*

Dan: Wasn't asked. Doing it off my own back. Going to meet potential new customer, a newsagent along the high street. Really need to cinch this! Miss you too x

Hmmkay, he misses me too. It's a start!

'So, she looks like a movie star? So what?' Becca shrugs, reaching down toward the play mat to put Noah's ungovernable sock back on during another late-morning mother and baby group coffee summit at the community centre.

'You mean, you wouldn't be bothered if your Jim was working with hot stuff eight and a half hours a day, five days a week?' I probe in disbelief.

'No, why would I?' she replies apathetically. 'The world is full of beautiful women and unless I was to keep Jim locked up 24/7, statistically there's always going to be situations when he's around one of them.'

I give a tepid nod.

'Besides,' she goes on, 'no sod would have him! There's only me stupid enough.'

Voice in head: *Wow. I am literally the Jim in my relationship!*

'The trouble is, I'm seriously punching with Dan.' I sigh, peering down at the toothpaste stain on my top, only then realising said top is inside-out as well as stained. Good God!

'Look, you don't know the first thing about this boss of his. How do you know she isn't married? I mean, fair play to him, your Dan is a bit of alright, but that doesn't mean he's going to melt every woman's butter,' Becca reasons. 'Besides, she's a professional. Don't you think it's pretty insulting to just assume off the bat that she's the type of person to run around seducing her staff?'

'You're right,' I mumble, biting my lip and looking at the twins. 'You're totally right.'

Becca sighs, looking at me seriously. 'Look,

has your Dan ever given you any reason not to trust him?'

'No.'

'And has he ever let on that he's not happy with you?'

'No, never.'

She frowns. 'Then I think the problem is less about him and more about you,' she says, basically confirming what, deep down, I already know.

'Ugh! I wish I could just flick a switch and not feel this way,' I groan, head in hands. 'I don't want to be the jealous wife.'

'Look, when was the last time you did something for yourself?' Becca prompts.

I suck my teeth in, thinking hard. 'I did move to America but since coming back, marrying Dan and having the twins ... I don't remember.'

'Right, there's your problem!' she exclaims. 'You've gotten stuck in a cycle of stay-at-home parenting and you've forgotten who you are!'

'But everything's about the twins. That's just how it is when you have kids, right?' I frown back at her.

'No, it isn't ... well, not unless your name's Sonia Wilcox!' Becca mumbles discreetly, nodding in her direction. My eyes follow to where Gobzilla herself is sat cross-legged on the floor reading *The*

Very Hungry Caterpillar to Eagle – but really to the whole room – in a deranged and grating voice.

'Why don't you arrange a date night for you and the hubby?' Becca suggests. 'You don't even have to go out if you can't afford it. Just pack the twins off to their grandparents' overnight, take a long soak, do a face mask, open a bottle of wine, then round the evening off with a romantic meal-for-two and some hanky-panky!'

I pause in thought for a moment, deciding not to spoil things with any mention of my creamy Tuscan chicken "special early grave" edition.

'Could work,' I say with a nod, picturing said romantic meal ending in frantic kitchen table sex.

Mental note: *Since want to shag husband rather than kill him, had better commission Tesco's Finest range for "shove in oven" convenience this time.*

'And Mother owes me a favour,' I add, a heartening smile creeping up my face.

'Now look, are you *sure* you can handle them for the whole night?' I ask Dad, mummy-guilt pricking as we jointly fix the twins' seats into the back of his car in the early afternoon that Friday.

'Of course we can! We were parents before you and Daniel, you know!' Mother scoffs from the front seat.

Yes, and I'm living proof that you made a shit job of it!

'Well, any problems, just give me a shout,' I urge, kissing the twins like it's the last time I'll ever see them again. 'No, no! Don't do that! Not the sad orphan faces,' I groan as the pair of them stare up at me with forlorn-looking baby blues, their expressions screaming 'No, Mummy! Don't leave us with Nanny Nut-Nut!'.

'Don't worry love, they'll be fine,' Dad soothes, patting my shoulder. 'Now, you both have a lovely, relaxing evening and we'll see you tomorrow.'

'Thanks, Dad. Bye.' I sniff as I stand shivering on the pavement, feeling like the star of this year's John Lewis Christmas tearjerker special as I wave the car off down the cold and frosty street till it's out of sight.

'Right, time for a little self-care,' I mumble out loud on my way back up to the flat, which already feels weird and empty without the twins. Peppa Pig blares away in the background, and I find myself pausing to watch as Daddy Pig accidentally turns on the shower and soaks himself on a train, before being forced to answer the door to the conductor dripping wet.

Wow. I can so relate!

Reluctantly prising myself away from Peppa Pig, I set about transforming the bathroom from a tumultuous, disorderly jumble of baby baths, rubber ducks and bath toys to a calming, contemplative, and zen-like spa retreat. I run the bath, adding a long glug of aromatherapy oil to it. Mmmm, heaven! A few candles around the bath, a face mask, some relaxing music and I'll be well on my way to peace and tranquillity!

'Perfect,' I sigh, breezing back into the bathroom, lighting three tealights and resting them on the bath's edge. 'Now all I need to do is hop in and let my cares melt away.'

I make off to the bedroom to undress as a thought crosses my mind. *Where did I put that Bluetooth speaker?*

Traipsing half-naked through to the front room, I locate it and launch a YouTube search for meditation music. With everything from ocean sounds to rain and thunderstorms, I find myself spoilt for choice! Making a random selection, I head back to the bathroom, speaker in hand, already feeling at ease from the relaxing crackling fire sounds … only, wait, what's that smell? And shit, is that smoke I see coming from the bathroom?

Racing toward the door, I find that the crackling fire sounds *aren't* from YouTube, they're bloody *real* and the only thing melting away is the fucking bathtub! *Oh*, and the shower curtain.

'HOLY FUUUCK!'

Dropping the speaker in shock, I tear through to the kitchen and frantically empty out the wash basin of dirty dishes. Panting, I turn on the taps full pelt and fill the basin with cold water, slopping it all over the place and almost skidding over backwards in my rush to get back to the bathroom.

Eyes bulging in panic, I chuck the water toward the flames in a careering great swoosh while soothing panpipe music blares away from the speaker lying abandoned on the bathroom floor, making for what is possibly the most unlikely soundtrack ever to all hell breaking loose!

The water reduces the flames but doesn't put them out completely. Squealing like a nutter, I climb onto the edge of the bath and tear down the shower pole, tossing it and the burning curtain into the bath water and watching as it instantly extinguishes with a smoky hiss.

'Thank God,' I sigh in relief, pleased with my quick-thinking, before, less than three seconds later, falling in after it head-first!

During my brief underwater struggle, I wonder:

a.   if Amber Ross has ever done similar (of course she fucking hasn't!)

b.   if Daddy Pig may be my cartoon counterpart

c.   how self-care became self-scare!

Great! So that's an hour lost since packing the twins off and all I've managed to do so far in my rare, child-free afternoon is set fire to the bloody place!

'So much for peace and tranquillity,' I huff, walking into the kitchen to find it flooded to fuck. I race to turn the taps off and then stand back in assessment, wondering how in the hell I've managed to stay alive these past thirty-one years.

∞∞∞

Having tidied up both messes and the rest of the flat to the best of my ability, I throw on a low-cut top and pair it with a leather-look midi skirt. I add a slick of lip gloss, a flick of mascara and several frantic pumps of the last dredges of my Jimmy Choo perfume. Hm, not quite the silhouette I was hoping for, but at least it's out-out glam.

Even though we'll be in-in, as always!

With a Tesco's Finest meal-for-two cooking away nicely in the oven – which is definitely on – I open a bottle of wine, but decide against lighting any more candles until there's a responsible adult at home.

After a couple of glasses, the stress of the day soon begins to ebb away. Ha! Who needs a long soak anyway when Blossom Hill does the job so much quicker?

Pretty soon, my thoughts turn to my marriage. We've got the night to ourselves, so what can I do to give Dan a welcome home he won't forget? Perhaps I could get to Dan's heart via his trousers? He *is* a man, after all, and what do men love just as much as food and beer? Sex, obviously! Granted, I'm not very good in that department either, but I could be! I mean, how hard must it be? Certainly not as hard as cooking from bloody scratch, I'm sure.

Brainwave: *Permanently empty ball sack = significantly reduced capacity to notice hot women.*

OMG, yes! That's it! If Dan's testosterone levels are dampened because he's getting so much sex at home, then he's not going to notice *her* as much. Why on earth didn't I think of this before?

Feeling fraudulently confident from the wine, I wiggle off my undies in initiation of my clever sexual masterplan.

Expectation:

1. *I sit seductively on sofa.*
2. *Dan comes in through door from hard*

day at work.

3. *Our eyes meet.*
4. *We say nothing.*
5. *I undertake "Sharon Stone leg cross".*
6. *Frantic sofa-sex follows.*
7. *Sex in general goes from once in blue moon to four times per week.*
8. *Dan only has eyes for me!*

Reality:

Memories of very similar scenario in million-dollar house in America – how was I to know Brian would be bringing his work partner back to the house that night anyway? – combined with repulsion at practice-run (now four stone heavier) means I am forced to get knickers back on at lightning speed before front door opens!

'What are you doing down there on the floor?' comes Dan's voice from in the doorway.

'Er, just dropped an earring,' I excuse, blushing.

He pulls a strange face as he steps inside and takes off his jacket. 'Oh. Are the twins in bed already?'

'No, er, Dad and Mother stopped by to collect them at lunchtime,' I tell him, rising to my feet. 'They're going to have them overnight so we can…'

Have mad sex!

'Er, you know, spend some time together,' I

tell him, brushing my hair out of my face awkwardly. 'I've made dinner!'

'Oh, right,' he says, not half as enthusiastically as I'd have liked – recent close brush with salmonella or not.

'Oh, er, not from scratch!' I cut in swiftly. 'It's one of those set meals, you know?'

He nods, visibly reassured. 'So, you've had the afternoon to yourself then,' he remarks, loosening his tie.

Yes, and I spent it starting fires and floods.

'Are you hungry?' I ask, giving a shady sideward glance.

'Well, Amber treated us all to pizza this afternoon, so not really,' he replies, patting his belly.

Great. After all that effort I went to pre-heating the oven, Margot's already fed him!

His face falls as he observes my unimpressed look. 'Why? You've not gone to any trouble.'

No. But the chefs behind Tesco's Finest range did!

I shrug, trying to hide my disappointment.

'I'm just gonna take a quick shower,' he announces, turning to walk off.

'No!' I roar, earning myself an even stranger look. I know I've got to fess up about the fire in the bathroom at some point, but I'd rather the confession was post-coital.

He frowns, freezing in place. 'Sorry?'

'Well, I've missed you,' I tell him, which isn't a lie. 'Can't we at least sit and have some wine together first? I've waited all day to see you.'

And who knows, if I can get enough Blossom Hill down him then we could end up in the shower together … and hopefully he'll be too pissed to notice both the bath and my bare arse.

'Okay, yeah. Let's have a drink together!' He smiles, following me into the kitchen.

'So, how was your day?' I ask.

'Oh, great as always,' he enthuses.

'That's good,' I reply through a lukewarm smile, handing him the biggest glass of wine you've ever seen in your life.

Now shut up and get it down you. And, yes, I am grooming you!

'I'll put some music on, shall I?' I chirp, walking over to the sound system in the lounge.

'Yeah, go for it,' he agrees, sitting himself down at the table.

I select a random ballads album and walk sultrily over to join him as Adele's dulcet tones ring out from the speakers.

'Amber *loves* Adele!' he remarks before my

arse has even touched the chair. 'She's been to see her six times.'

'Has she?' I mumble indifferently.

'Yeah, she's a superfan!'

'Oh, right,' I murmur, trying to resuscitate my come-to-bed smile.

Er, hello from the other side of the table! I haven't packed the twins off for the night so you can sit and talk about your hot new boss, you know.

'So, er, do you think you'll pass your probation period?' I ask.

'Well, Amber says I'm a breath of fresh air, so I reckon so!' He beams.

'Well in that case maybe we should make an appointment with a mortgage adviser,' I suggest, steering the conversation back to us.

'Well actually, I read in my new starter pack that they offer one-to-one financial advice at work. I could ask Amber about it on Mond—'

'No, let's just go to the bank like everyone else!' I snap, blood pressure surging.

He frowns, holding his hands up and staring across the table at me as though I'm a psycho.

Pfft! He should've seen me earlier when I was running around naked, extinguishing fires to panpipe music. He hasn't even seen psycho!

As we sip our drinks in a lingering silence,

I conclude that frantic kitchen table sex is looking wildly ambitious.

'Alright, what's wrong?' he asks eventually, placing his wine glass a little too hard on the table for my liking.

I shrug. 'Why should anything be wrong?'

'Come on, Lizzie. I know that face! You've got a monk on about something.'

I take a deep breath. 'Well, to be honest with you, I'd organised tonight hoping that we could spend some quality time together as a couple. But so far all you've done is talk about work,' I huff, stopping short of telling him that I've looked his new boss up on LinkedIn and know full well she's an eleven out of ten.

'Oh?' he remarks, looking taken aback. 'Well it's a new job. I would've thought it was only natural that I bring it up now and again?'

The job, fine! The delectable Amber Ross, so not fine!

I stare back at him, mouth twitching, lost for words. I can't very well tell him how much I object to him eating pizza and discussing Adele's back catalogue with total babes while I spend my days nappy changing and nanny napping. The plan was to seduce him, not to show him that of all the hot women in the world he went and married The Gruffalo!

'Are you okay?' he asks, looking concerned. 'Is it that time of the month?'

Ooh, that's done it!

'Oh! So women never get miffed about anything in life and if they do it means they're premenstrual?' I bark.

'I never meant it like that. I just wondered if that might be the reason,' he counters. 'I can't think why else you'd be so touchy.'

'You should probably go have your shower.' I sigh, rising from my chair and storming off to top up my wine.

'Wow! What did I do?!' he exclaims, shaking his head in my wake.

List of things he did not do:

1. Compliment me on my appearance, even if it's a million miles off Margot Robbie standard.
2. Give me my hello kiss.
3. Tell me he'd missed me too.
4. Ask me how my day was.

Hm. Am not ready to fess up about man made natural disasters in flat, so scrap that one!

5. Stop talking about Amber effing Ross!

Just as I wonder whether the evening could be saved by walking into the bedroom, saying nothing and shoving him onto the bed for frantic make-up sex—

'Jesus Christ, Lizzie! What the hell's happened in the bathroom?!'

Ahem!

Chapter 11:

Crappy Birthday

Instagram influencer's birthday: *Entire front room decked out in rose gold banners, bunting and enormous, confetti-filled helium balloons. Gifting table crammed with cards, gift bags and beautifully wrapped gifts. Birthday girl standing among it all in ultra-short, trendy nightwear, holding age-specific balloon and grinning from ear to ear. No further validation needed that she is loved. She is special. She is celebrated.*

My birthday: *Business as usual.*

Well, other than for a single card from Dan and the twins that was left on the coffee table early this morning with the vague promise of "a few surprises this evening", a handful of early-morning Facebook greetings from people I never speak to, and Mother's annual call to remind me that thirty-two years ago to the day, I gave her the most painful and humiliating experience of her life – with the penultimate worst, Uncle Tony's pissing up the new conservatory, coming in a close second!

'Dreadful experience … *dreadful!*' she chir-rups down the line. 'That's why you're an only child, dear. You were hefty and stubborn even in the womb! The consultant had to practically drag you out with his forceps!'

'Yes, I know, Mother. I swear you tell me this every year!'

Bugger me, thirty-two years of reminders that I'm a born pain in the arse! Validation, you say? Validation?!

'Daddy has put some pennies into your bank from us, dear, so that you can get whatever you like,' she announces, going on to tell me exactly what I should buy with them.

'Now, then!' she continues, not letting me or my date of birth dominate the conversation for a second more than it must. 'Daddy and I will be around first thing Friday morning to drop Horatio off to you. Then we can get away nice and early for our little hiatus!'

A sudden sense of doom washes over me as I recall my promise to Mother. It always seems like a good idea giving in to people just to get them to sod off, till they rock up for the goods. I close my eyes in dread, clutching the receiver as Mother hangs up on me in the usual way.

I proceed to while away the daytime hours

with my thoughts divided between wondering how I'm going to fit an out-of-control, incontinent hound into my insane life for a week, and what Dan might've got me for my birthday.

Flowers? *Maybe.*

Jewellery? *Possibly.*

Sexy underwear? *Unlikely, but hats off to him if he manages to find some to fit me!*

By 2pm I conclude that the florist van probably isn't coming, cut my losses and turn up the television I'd muted for the past six hours so as to be able to hear the buzzer. Dan always used to send me flowers before we were married. These days, he doesn't seem to bother.

Inner voice of reason: *Perhaps he's going to give you some flowers in person?*

Inner twat: *Meh! Nothing beats the excitement of a florist van drawing up outside your house.*

Don't get me wrong, I'm not someone who measures a happy marriage with florist bouquets received per annum, but if he gives me flowers in person then I don't get to put on my Oscar winner's acceptance face for the delivery man, and nor shall the neighbours get to see that I'm "worth it" like L'Oréal! Bugger.

Later...

A text! I've got a text!

Dan: *Babe, going to be a little late. Be home as soon as! x*

Inner twat: *He's having it off with Margot on my birthday!*

Inner voice of reason: *Dan never lets me down. He'd never willingly come home late on my birthday; not when he knows how badly I'd kick off. He must have something pretty special planned!*

Eeeeeek! Yes, that's got to be it! He's planned something amazing! But what, though? Clearly, he's bringing the surprise home! OMG, how exciting!

7.10 pm

He's still not home! I don't believe it! He left at 7am and it's now after 7pm. *Twelve whole hours* on my own – not counting the twins – in the flat on my birthday and clearly he couldn't care less. He'd rather be with her! He's off screwing her. I know it! I've known it from day one! Oh, there's his key in the door—

I quickly straighten up on the sofa in anticipation as the door opens and he scrambles through it, weighed down with carrier bags.

'Hey, happy birthday!' he greets me, catching his breath. 'So sorry I'm late, babe. Had to make it to the shops during rush hour, didn't I?'

Ignoring the stroppy little voice in my head

bawling that, fundamentally, he's had 364 days to plan my birthday, I force a smile and resist the urge to leap up from the sofa and start rummaging through the bags.

'Right. Back in a minute,' he announces with a wink that would otherwise have been shivery-sexy if I wasn't so miffed.

Moments later, I hear the sound of Sellotape coming from the bedroom. You've got to be kidding me? Is he seriously in there wrapping the gifts while I sit here on the sofa waiting for them?

Around ten minutes later, he returns and places a dozen presents wrapped in shiny gold gift wrap onto the coffee table. My face lights up. Wow! Twelve fat presents to open. The boy did good!

'Happy birthday ... *again*!' He smiles, leaning across for a peck before I open the first. I can't help but feel slightly swindled that they were only just wrapped moments ago. I mean, yeah, they still count as presents but, Christ, the Sellotape has barely even had time to stick!

'*Oh!* Percy Pig sweets!' I chuckle, placing them back down onto the coffee table. 'You know me so well!'

He nods fervently. 'Go on, open the next!'

I smile in anticipation, selecting another gift from the table. '*Oh!* Percy Pig chocolate coins,' I nod, feeling a bit like a five-year-old.

'They've got them in for Christmas,' he reveals excitedly.

I nod, not quite matching his exuberant grin. Yes, I'm a chocolate lover. Heck, I've even been known to eat dog chocolate as a kid, but chocolate moments are best enjoyed staring into space, not battling to pick off the foil casings on chocolate coins. Still, mustn't be ungrateful now, must we?

I give the next gift a prod. Hm, interesting! Feels like a posh smellies set if I'm not mistaken...

'*Oh.* A giant Percy Pig chocolate figurine,' I remark impassively.

'Yeah!' he enthuses, looking really pleased for me.

'Um ... is this a joke?' I half laugh, hoping to God it *is* as I unwrap the twelfth and final gift to find yet another consecutive item of Percy Pig confectionary.

Bugger me, I must have the entire bloody range by now!

'Why would it be a joke?' Dan responds, straight-faced.

'I mean ... is that it? Is that all you've got me?' I frown under knitted brows, stopping short of asking where my real gifts are and half expecting Ant and Dec to jump out with a bloody camera crew.

He stares vacantly at me for a few moments. 'Oh! Not entirely, just a sec,' he announces, reaching for a carrier bag beside the sofa and whipping out a large box which he holds out proudly in front of me. 'Surprise!'

Great. He's only gone and got me the effing birthday cake as well!

'Ah,' I remark with a limp smile.

'Well, you could look a bit more grateful. Cost a packet, that lot!' he laughs.

I stare back at him in the midst of a sort of perplexed inner turmoil at the thought of the untold options of non-Percy Pig items he could've bought for the same amount of money.

'Okay, what's wrong?' he sighs wearily. 'I thought you liked Percy Pig?'

'I do, but the entire range? *Seriously?!*'

He shrugs. 'Well, if you like it then why not?'

'I do like other things in life besides sweets, though,' I hint, aggrieved that he must look at me as some kind of walking, sweet-eating machine to expect me to be nothing less than lit with my present pile. 'I mean, you basically finished work, rushed to M&S and bought them out of Percy Pigs for me. It's not very thoughtful, is it?'

'Well, what were you expecting?' he frowns, scratching his head.

I stare back at him, aghast. *Yes*, a few items of confectionary are always welcome in anyone's gift pile, but an absolute shit tonne of children's sweets and nothing else for a thirty-two-year-old woman who struggles with her weight? It's totally tone-deaf! I mean, I'll eat them. God knows, I'll eat them – and feel like a giant sea turtle when I next take a bath – but that's not the style of the Dan I know and love. It's not my Mr Wonderful, the archetypal romantic and shining example to all men. I don't understand it. He's usually really thoughtful and considerate. Something's different. Something's changed in him. It's like he doesn't even care anymore.

Astonished, I say nothing.

As Dan storms off to the bedroom shaking his head, I find myself alone once again and questioning everything. They do say that marriage and kids is the biggest test of any relationship, but I've always thought of it as more of a blessing than a burden. Up until now, I thought Dan felt the same. Back at the beginning, he had a way of making me feel like I was the centre of his universe. Granted, things change and we're both growing all the time. Is it a case that, rather than grow together, we've been growing apart? Or is it something else? I don't know. But it has to be said that there does seem to be a patently obvious Amber Ross-shaped link in all of this!

∞∞∞

'You seriously think he's having an affair?' Becca frowns across the table at the community centre the next morning.

'Oh, everything points to it,' I declare with a grave headshake, peeling back the foil on yet another Percy Pig chocolate coin. 'There's so much I could tell you.'

'Go on then,' she prompts expectantly, sipping her coffee as mine sits going as cold as my sex life.

'Well,' I begin, drawing in a deep, preparatory breath and glancing at the twins, 'he's getting home later and later from work. He takes his phone everywhere with him, including to the toilet. I mean, he more or less bit my head off the other day when I asked to borrow it to call the health visitor while we were out food shopping. Gave me a proper lecture about keeping my own properly charged and made some crappy excuse about expecting an important call so he didn't have to hand it over,' I reveal.

'Then there's the lack of thought. Being unusually inconsiderate, especially with the charade last night on my birthday. Plus, he hasn't touched me in weeks. And we don't seem to talk anymore. Honestly, we used to lie in bed discussing everything from tax codes to alien invasions. Now all he ever talks about is work and *her!* I'm telling you, Becca, those are some pretty sure-fire signs, don't you think?'

'Hm, maybe,' she murmurs pensively. 'One dead giveaway is when they start making more of an effort than usual with their appearance. You know, going to the gym, wearing aftershave and stuff. Have you noticed any of that?' she probes.

'Well, he's a personal trainer, so he's always been a gym buff. And he *always* smells great,' I reply, almost disappointed that they can't be counted as clues.

Mental note: *Am not Vera or similar case-cracking ace. Am spurned wife. And this is own husband am talking about. This is not exciting!*

'Is he showering more than usual?' Becca asks.

'Well, he always seems to shower straight after work every night without fail,' I reveal.

'Shit. That doesn't sound good.' She grimaces. 'Not to be gross, but even quickies are messy. If you were a bloke, what's the first thing you'd do after?'

I shrug, rolling the empty coin foil between my fingers. 'Roll over and start snoring?'

'Besides that,' she sniggers.

'Well, give my piece a wash, I suppose.'

She bites her lip and lets the silence do the talking.

Voice in head: *OMG, they've been at it at work! He's probably had her everywhere: in the toilets, on the photocopier, in her car – in our car, even! Hell! I might've been sitting in Amber Ross's love juice all this time and been none the wiser!*

'Look, Becca. Tell me now and tell me true. Do *you* think he's cheating on me?' I plead across the table.

'Well, from what you've said, my first guess is he's shafting her, yeah,' she answers blithely.

I freeze, bottom lip trembling. Looks like I wasn't quite ready to have my suspicions confirmed by a second party.

'Look, Lizzie. At the end of the day, it doesn't matter what I or anyone else thinks about all this. The only person to talk to is Dan. *He's* the only one who can give you the answers.'

Before I can utter a word, Gobzilla appears at the side of our table, sporting an insane grin. 'So, Eagle is now fully toilet trained and he doesn't even turn three until January!' she crows, giving credence to my viewpoint that those who start sentences with 'so' are almost always annoying, punchable people in general.

'He's ever so good! Tells me right away when he wants to go pee-pee or poo-poo. And it's meant so much less washing for me, you know? Because I only ever used cloth nappies. We like to do our bit for the planet. And of course, less washing means less electric. So it's cool beans!'

I force a smile. I mean, good for her, but my frazzled brain isn't quite up to speed yet. The conversation has literally skyrocketed from Dan's infidelity to Eagle's urinary tract and bowels in 0.5 seconds!

'In fact, he's taken to it so well that he doesn't even need pyjama pants at night,' she squeals delightedly.

Well I give that a couple of days at best, after which point I imagine she'll have a hefty electric bill and the worst carbon footprint in Britain!

'Our health visitor says he's the earliest she's known,' she boasts, ignoring our complete lack of response. 'We think he's going to be super-advanced, don't we, buddy?' She beams down at him. 'Eagle? Eagle, what are you doing?' she asks, her frown at odds with her sing-song voice.

He stares into space, his tongue resting on his bottom lip and one arm fumbling around his back – not looking all that super-advanced, it has to be said.

She sighs. 'What are you hiding? Have you been pinching snacks from the tables again?'

Eagle draws his arm out from behind him

and holds out a nugget of his own waste. Sonia lets out a mortified shriek and slaps his hand, causing Exhibit A to roll off and drop to the wooden floor with a muted *donk*.

Becca and I look on open-mouthed as she forages red-faced in her almighty backpack, brings out a tissue, scoops up Exhibit A, then forcibly grabs and drags Eagle away by his arm without another word.

'Did that seriously just happen?' I murmur in wide-eyed disbelief.

Chapter 12:

Doggin' Around

'Horatio, heel! Heel at once!' comes Mother's ear-splitting rasp through the intercom early on Friday morning.

Forget being carted off to Azkaban, if ever there were a perfect time for the Dumbledore phoenix clap, it's here and now!

'Come straight up,' I instruct through a lazily disguised sigh.

Why in the hell did I agree to this? That dog is a disaster. *I'm* a bloody disaster! Nothing good can come from this, which is a sentiment confirmed instantly upon opening the front door to discover Horatio on his tod, sniffing the corridor carpet with his lead trailing behind him and no sign of any owner at the end of it.

Craning my neck toward the stairs, I catch the tail-end of Dad and Mother's conversation ascending upwards.

'—bloody dog is a law unto itself. I'm telling

you now, Petunia, there's only so much more I can take before it ends up in Battersea Dogs Home!'

'Oh, gooooood! Well, why don't you give them a call and ask if they've a place for you too while you're at it!'

Ouch.

'Ah. There you are, dear!' Mother greets me in the usual way.

'Morning,' I reply dispiritedly.

'Here's your birthday card for Wednesday,' she announces, flourishing a pale pink envelope toward me. 'I would have posted it out to you the day before, but there was just too much to do this week before we go away,' she complains.

And flinging our only child's birthday card into one of several post boxes we would've passed along the way simply wasn't on our list of priorities, dear.

'I've had the hairdressers, a manicure, a pedicure, and I've had to go and fetch our currency.' She sighs. 'Daddy had the car to clean and vacuum out, then there was the lawn to feed before winter gets underway and, ugh, the plants! I'm telling you now, my chrysanthemums have never been the same since that awful man collapsed on them. Then there was the packing to do and all Horatio's things to get together! Goodness, I shall need another holiday just to get over all the preparation for this one!'

Remind me never to retire. Sounds fatiguing!

'Did you do anything nice for your birthday, dear?' she asks, airily.

'No, not r—'

'Oh, how nice! Now then, come here, Horatio! Come and meet your new mummy for the week!' she bawls.

OMG, a week. A bloody week! *I'm not even sure I can last an hour*, I think to myself, peering down at the daft mutt who is panting and prancing about like a pony.

'Listen, I'm not gonna lie, I'm a bit worried about his lack of training,' I confess, looking to Mother for some assurance.

'Oh, he's perfectly toilet trained, dear,' she reasons with a dismissive wave of the hand.

'I was actually thinking more in terms of discipline,' I correct with a deflated sigh.

'Secret is to walk him a lot. Knacker him out!' Dad winks over her shoulder.

All well and good when you're retired, but what if you haven't the time to fart?

'Now, here's his doggy bag,' Mother announces, thrusting an enormous Cath Kidston floral travel bag at me. 'I'm afraid that, like Mummy, he doesn't travel light, dear! But you'll have everything you need in there, everything you'll need. I've written out a list of instructions so that you can keep to his routine.'

'Stuff it's routine! It can FIFO as far as I'm concerned,' I grunt, not expecting her to be listening.

She pulls an addled expression. 'First in, first out? Isn't that to do with calculating taxes, dear?'

I stop short of enlightening her that I'd actually meant "fit in or fuck off".

'Now, I'll just pop in and see the babies,' she trills, barging into the flat.

'So, are you looking forward to getting away?' I ask Dad as he shuffles inside.

'Well, I'm not really getting away, am I?' he reminds me, nodding toward Mother who already has Jack in tears.

'Oh, Elizabeth, you've made these children strange! It doesn't pay to mollycoddle them, dear, it really doesn't. I mean, look at him! You'd think the world has ended just because his Grandma's picked him up!' she accuses.

Dad and I exchange knowing sideward glances, as Mia predictably follows her brother's lead within seconds. Well, they do say children are great judges of character!

'Heavens above! Would you listen to that chorus?! Thank goodness we're going away, dear. I'd be tearing my hair out if I had to endure this all day.'

'They'll be quiet as mice once you've left,' I blurt without thinking.

'Come on, Desmond, we'd best be awf. The French Riviera is calling … I can hear it, dear!' she chirrups excitedly, staring into the distance with a crazed grin. 'We'll call you once we've arrived and unpacked, see how Horatio's settling in. And, if you get a chance, dear, pop online to that Tube place. I've got my own channel! Uncle Gerald set it all up for me last week for payment in duty-free cigars.'

'But what could *you* possibly offer YouTube viewers?' I frown in dismay.

'Oh, all sorts!' she chortles patronisingly, as though she, having only just discovered YouTube, now knows far more about it than I do. 'People love nothing more than to sit and nose at other people's holidays, dear.'

'Do they?' I shrug, not believing for a moment that I'm the only person in the world who objects to ten-minutely updates on socials from people reminding everyone they're on holiday.

'D'ohhhhhh, there's no end to the sort of material I could be making!' Mother booms, making me jump. 'There's housekeeping, cake-making, cookery, home entertaining,' she sings. 'You can do what they call live streams, dear. It's where people tune into you live from all over the world. Uncle

Gerald says there's a fortune to be made from it all. You never know, if my channel takes off then Auntie Val might not be the only one with a little place out in the sun!'

Shit me. Mother, a YouTube star? Whatever will she think of next?!

'Anyway, we'd best be awf,' she repeats. 'Desmond! Get that GoPro at the ready, dear. I'd like to film us setting off for the airport.'

Dad smiles sympathetically 'Bye then, love. Hope you get on okay,' he says, patting my shoulder on his way out.

'And don't forget to give our snaps a big thumbs-up on Bookface!' Mother chortles, gliding through the front door and ending up wedged in it as Horatio makes a sudden dash for freedom. 'No, you *cannot* come to the French Riviera! You're staying here, dog!' she scolds, pushing him back inside by the nose. 'Well, don't just stand there, Desmond, give me a hand!' she yells, engaged in a battle of wills that the dog is definitely winning.

Battle eventually won and farewells bid, I find myself engaged in a staring contest with the bloody thing as it sits by the door looking down its nose at me.

'Now, let's get one thing straight, mutt,' I grunt, wagging my finger sternly. 'You're in *my* territory now, and I ain't your mummy for the week – I'm your master!'

Ten minutes later....

'Dan! You've got to help me! We're trapped in the bedroom!'

'Look, Lizzie, I can't come home every time there's a bloody spider in the flat!' he retorts listlessly down the line.

'It's not a spider, it's Horatio!' I hiss into the handset.

'Dog, spider, whatever! I still can't leave work.' He sighs. 'Anyway, what's the problem?'

'He's been chasing me around the flat and biting my ankles! I've had to barricade us in the bedroom for our own safety. Honestly, Dan, the bloody thing's nuts! It wants blood! I swear to God!'

'Well, have you tried feeding it?' he offers limply.

'Well, according to Mother's *War and Peace* instructions, he's not due to be fed until this evening,' I explain, grabbing and scanning through the ridiculous dossier laying in a heap on the bed beside me.

'Well, what do you expect me to do about it? I'm at work, Lizzie! I'm not supposed to be taking or making calls outside of breaks,' he snaps.

'But ... but it's an emergency! How am I going to get anything done for the twins? How will

I go to the bathroom?!' I plead in panic.

He snorts in dismay. 'Well, I don't bloody know! You'll just have to deal with it till I get home. Assert some control. Look, I've got to go. Love you, bye.'

Voice in head: *Yeah, you'd best get back to Ambs. Hurry now, before her minge goes cold!*

So that's it, is it? He's left me to the dogs! He has quite literally left me to the dogs! And, as sod's law would have it, I really need a wee.

With a twin on each hip, I tiptoe tentatively toward the bedroom door, pausing and putting my ear to it.

'Where are you, you little f...' I begin to say through the lock. Mummy-guilt pricks as the twins babble away at me. I've been trying not to swear in front of them from early on – you know, starting as we mean to go on – but what bloody chance do I stand with this sort of carry on?

Pushing down the door handle with my elbow – a totally underrated body part I've leant on heavily since having twins – I inch open the door and peer through the gap, breathing heavy and heart pounding. Wow, this is just like *Dog Soldiers*, only with a single crazed corgi as the enemy rather than a pack of werewolves.

Eyes on the open bathroom door, I decide to make a dash for it but hesitate partway as it dawns on me that the enemy is nowhere to be seen.

'Oh!' I exclaim, pleasantly surprised and daring to believe that he might've given up and gone off somewhere to chase his tail.

Tiptoeing through to the front room, I discover him filthy and panting, lying on the sofa with one of my bras from the toppled airer on his head and our giant Bird of Paradise plant on its side nearby.

This is quite possibly going to be the longest week of my life!

∞ ∞ ∞

'I'm not sure I can go on,' I announce at the kitchen table next morning, head in my hands.

'Don't say things like that!' Dan snaps from over by the fridge, looking horrified.

'I meant in terms of having that bloody dog!' I scoff, eyeing it resentfully as it wolfs its breakfast like it's never been fed. 'I'm tempted to stick it in a kennel till next Friday and pay for it myself. Mother need never find out.'

'If we had that sort of cash spare, I'd say go for it,' Dan mutters, swiping his water bottle from the countertop and turning to leave.

'Hang on, could you not take the dog with

you on your run?' I suggest, face lighting up at the prospect of five minutes' peace.

'What? Take that thing out running? No way, Lizzie! I'm meeting a client at the park at ten,' he says with a snort on his way out of the kitchen.

'It's just that Dad said the trick is to knacker him out. A 5 km would totally do that,' I argue, following him to the front door. 'Then we won't have to keep hiding from him in the wardrobe!'

'Lizzie, people pay me to run alongside them as their coach. They don't pay me to run alongside them with your mum's dog to knacker it out because it's a pain in the arse!' he protests, his tone suggesting that the matter is non-negotiable and the subject closed.

'Alright, whatever.' I shrug as he gives me the briefest of pecks on the forehead before he disappears out the door.

Mental note: *Wow, all I did was ask him to take the dog and he near enough bit my head off! Maybe he's not going to the park to meet a client at all. Maybe, just maybe, he's sneaking off to meet her!*

Plodding back into the kitchen with a face like a wet weekend, I flip the switch down on the kettle to make a cuppa. Before the water's even tepid, I've decided that there's something far more urgent I need to do.

'Calm down, arsehead, or I'm not taking you any-where again!' I threaten, as Horatio forcibly pulls me and the pram down the street in the direction of the park.

Now, we're only here because I thought we could all benefit from a nice morning walk with me dressed from head to toe in black, a baseball cap and crap black Terminator sunglasses. I mean, if Dan's there and we spot him then it'll put my mind at rest. And if he's not then I'll know for sure he's lied to me.

'Slow down, you nutter!' I bark at the dog while yanking up the waist of my black joggers which seem surprisingly loose compared to when I last wore them.

Mental note: *Wow! Must be losing weight!*

Follow-up note: *Or could just be absence of enormous baby bump. Meh!*

As we enter through the gates of the park, I begin scanning various spandex-clad fitness fan-atics in a Terminator-like manner:

Male runner. Fair-haired. Aged 35 – 40. Defin-itely not Dan!

Female runner, age 28 – 30, size six. Definitely doesn't eat Hula Hoop sandwiches!

We walk further and further through the park with no sign of Dan, nor any supposed fitness client. I glance at my watch and see that it's only 10.03 am. He said he was meeting his client at ten, so unless he's meeting Mo Farah the pair of them ought to still be around somewhere.

Voice in head: *He's lied to me. I knew it! I could tell from the way he was so touchy about not taking Horatio. After all, when you're off planting the parsnip, the last thing you'd want is that arse of a dog tagging along.*

As we pass the pond, my mind busy imagining all sorts, Horatio makes a mad lunge at a flock of geese preening themselves by the water's edge. An almighty cacophony of squawking, flapping and barking suddenly erupts out of nowhere. It takes me a moment to realise that he's pulling me and the pram along with him and if I don't act quickly then we'll all be going for a swim in around three seconds!

In panic, I slam the brake on the pram which stops it abruptly, sending me flying off to the left and belly diving to the ground, still clutching the lead in my fist. I skid across the gravel on my belly as the dog drags me along behind him.

'Heeeeellllllp!' I bawl in a tremored voice, screwing my eyes tightly shut and bracing myself for an almighty splash. Thankfully a passerby comes to my aid right in the nick of time, grabs the lead and manages to contain the dog.

Stunned, I remain on the ground on my

belly briefly. Then I notice the cold air on my legs and arse cheeks. Shit, my jogging bottoms! They've come down! Moving quicker than I ever have in my life, I pull them back up again.

Looking up, I lock eyes with Dan as he and his male client glide past me, the latter gawping open-mouthed.

Oh dear.

∞∞∞

'I would've stopped to help you up, but once I'd seen that the twins were alright I didn't want to embarrass you *or* my client … or myself,' Dan explains over a hot drink back at the flat. 'It was easier all round just to keep running.'

'How did you even know it was me? I had a cap and sunglasses on,' I point out, reflecting on the irony that *both* stayed on during the kerfuffle while my jogging bottoms forsook me.

'I recognised the dog first, then your pants,' he reveals matter-of-factly.

I close my eyes in shame, trying not to think too hard about how that might've looked.

'So, er, was there a reason for the Arnie shades?' Dan asks, visibly trying not to laugh.

'Not really, no,' I grimace through pursed

lips.

To think that I was supposed to be incognito. That's a bloody laugh!

'Where are you going?' I ask, watching as he gets up from the table.

'Just gonna take quick a shower,' he replies. 'Oh, and Lizzie? I'llllll be back!'

Chapter 13:

Bonnie & Clyde

'**I**'ve had over a thousand subscribers already, dear, and I've not been on there five minutes! Fabulous, isn't it? Anyway, how are you getting on? Have you found it?' Mother chivvies. This was meant to be an urgent call I'd made to discuss the dog, but has now somehow evolved to her blathering on about her YouTube channel.

'What's it called again?' I sigh, finger poised over the search bar on the app.

'"Come with Petunia",' she announces in a plummy voice.

'Christ, who came up with that? Sounds smutty!' I gasp, earning a puzzled look from Dan.

She tuts. 'Nonsense! It clearly points to travel. And it was Uncle Gerald's suggestion. He said a name like that would get me inundated with subscribers, and he wasn't wrong, was he? Anyhow, have you found it?'

'No, it's not appearing in the search results for some reason,' I say, scrolling through the top few accounts with no luck.

'Ah, well you've probably got the spelling wrong!' "Come" has been purposefully spelt the trendy way, as in C-U-M, dear,' she enlightens me, cool as a cucumber.

I almost choke on my own saliva. 'Come again?'

'Oh, well you know these whippersnappers and their insistence on shortening words!' she gabbles. 'Uncle Gerald said it was a must for maximum revenue.'

'But Mother, you can't possibly—'

'Have you found it yet, dear?' she cuts in over me. 'You'll know when you have because you'll see me on the thumbnail.'

'Er, yeah,' I mutter, eyes immediately drawn to what has to be her maddest close-up yet.

'Well go on then, like and subscribe!' she badgers like a seasoned YouTuber.

'Right. Done.' I sigh, wondering if I'll ever get the chance to speak.

'Tell her!' Dan mouths at me from over on the sofa.

I draw in a deep breath in readiness to drop the bombshell that we can no longer look after the dog.

'Now, how do I go about acquiring one of those grey ticks?' she cuts in quickly. 'Nigella Lawson has one and I'd rather like one too.'

'Oh, you can't. They're only for VIPs. Public figures and that.'

'Yes, dear, that's precisely why I'd like one,' she reveals excitably.

'Er, you can't, Mother. You're not a VIP or a public figure,' I remind her.

'Well, I do mix in wide circles, dear. There's not many in our parts who don't know the name. There's *bound* to be someone at YouTube who's heard of me,' she chortles.

'Listen Mother, about the dog—'

'Ooooooh! I've got another subscriber!' she squeals over me.

'I'm pretty sure that was me just now, Moth—'

'They can't get enough of me!' she gasps dramatically enough to earn an eye roll from Dan … and she's not even on speaker.

'Mother, please! I really have to talk to you about Horatio!' I yell desperately.

'Oh. How is he, dear?' she asks airily.

'Not good! He's trashed the flat and almost drowned me in less than twenty-four hours,' I reveal.

'Oh, that's good dear!' she chirrups. 'Now, I must go. I'm doing a live in five minutes to chat with my subscribers and get some viewer suggestions for content they'd like to see while we're here. Adieuuu!'

An erratic scrabble ensues, quickly followed by the hum of the dial tone.

'Well, what did she say? Are they going to pay for boarding at the kennels?' Dan asks.

'No they're not,' I reply numbly.

'*What?!* But we can't cope another day with him! When I took him out on his toilet walk last night, he bit my arse all the way home!'

'Yes, well I'd planned to tell her all of that, but I couldn't get a word in edgeways.' I shrug. 'She just kept on about her bloody YouTube channel, then she said she was doing a live in five minutes and—'

'Right,' he mutters, grabbing his phone out of his pocket.

'You're not calling her?' I frown.

'No, I'm going to join the live and tell her to sort her bloody dog out!' he replies with a scowl.

'No, Dan! Why don't I call Dad instead? He actually listens when people speak to him.'

'Yes, but *she* doesn't listen to him when he

speaks to her, so it's pointless! This way's easier. She'll be sat there waiting for comments so it's the best way to get through to her,' he reasons. 'Besides, I've got to see this. I could do with a laugh. What's the channel called again?'

'"Come With Petunia",' I reluctantly enlighten him. 'C-U-M.'

Dan laughs. 'Don't be daft. Come on, what is it?'

'That's it, I swear!' I insist, wide-eyed. 'Go on, search for it and you'll see for yourself.'

'If this is one of your silly wind ups,' he mutters, launching the search. And then...

'Holy shit!' he exclaims, eyes out on stalks around three seconds later.

'See!' I chuckle, joining him on the sofa.

'What was she thinking naming her channel something like that? It's pure smut! Why didn't you say something?'

'I did but she wouldn't listen! She thinks it's just a trendy shortened spelling,' I protest.

'Er, Lizzie, I think this influx of subscribers she's had might be under the impression that it's some sort of clandestine porn channel.' Dan gulps, clearly traumatised at the thought.

'I think you might be right,' I agree, just as the top of Mother's head appears on the screen, completely filling it.

'Is it on?! Is it on?!' comes her distorted bawl, the screen wobbling wildly as she grapples with the camera. She takes a step back and stands staring disturbingly into God knows how many people's screens who, to be fair, are probably staring at *her* in the exact same way.

'Ah, good, it's on!' she announces, face lifting. 'Well, hellooo! And a very warm welcome to the channel!' she trills, patting down her hair. 'I'm Petunia Bradshaw and I've decided to document my comings and goings for your viewing pleasure.'

Dan and I exchange uneasy glances.

'Now, then, I'd like to start by saying a big thank you to all my wonderful subscribers thus far for supporting the channel.' She beams a gummy grin, blowing a kiss at the camera. 'This week, we're over in Nice on the Cote d'Azur, and it's my ambition to give you as up close and personal an experience as possible! So do make sure you tell me what you'd like to see.'

I watch open-mouthed as the viewer count soars by the second.

'Now then! Let's see who we've got with us,' she chirps, peering down the screen. 'Ah! Hello to Buster Cherry! Now, that sounds like a very American name. Goodness me, viewers from across the pond already?! Desmond, they're only viewing me in the States!'

I glance down at so-called Buster's comment which simply reads, 'Hot,' accompanied by several fire emojis.

'Yes, Buster, we've been very lucky because it's extraordinarily warm for the time of year,' Mother replies, clueless. 'Do keep the comments coming!'

'U Wet?' comes another, this time from a Phil McCrackin.

'No, Phil, fortunately we've not had any rain during the trip so far.' She grins into the camera. 'But I'm sure it's very wet where you are in Scotland. Usually is!'

'PICS PLS,' comes another, all in caps.

'Ohhhh, yes! There'll be plenty of photographs, plenty of photographs! You can bank on it,' she trills delightedly.

'How long do you think it's going to be till the penny drops?' Dan sniggers.

'God knows,' I murmur in disbelief.

'Anyhow, let's have some suggestions for content you'd like to see. You know, places of interest *etcetera*,' Mother announces, clapping her hands.

'How about a tour of the nether regions?' a suggestion from Ben Dover pops up.

'Well, we've a wine tasting experience in

Toulon on Monday, which I'd be more than happy to film for you, Ben,' she replies, all smiles.

'Topless rollerblading along the Promenade des Anglais!' comes another, instantly wiping the silly grin off her face.

'Good grief, somebody always has to lower the tone, don't they?' she scowls into the camera. 'Well, we shall treat *that* with the contempt it deserves. Next?!'

'I AM HAPPY TO SEE BOBBS,' comes another misspelt special.

'Bobbs?' Mother frowns. 'Well, I can't say I've ever heard of the place. Perhaps our tour guide would know.'

And finally, the straw that breaks the camel's back: 'PLS SHOW TITTIES,' accompanied by several praying emojis.

'Right, that's it. Turn it off, Desmond! Turn it off at once! Now ... *NOW!*' she roars as an explosion of dislikes and swear emojis erupt on the screen from disappointed, randy viewers across the globe.

And then blackness.

Thanks to Dan's ingenuity, namely tying Horatio by his lead to his treadmill with the pace set at a constant 5 mph, we enjoy a far calmer rest of the week and somehow I make it to Friday's parole with my sanity just about intact!

Then I receive a frantic call from Dad first thing.

'Hello, love. Listen, we've hit a bit of a rut,' he pants, his tone unusually anxious.

'What is it? What's wrong?' I gulp, imagining all sorts.

'We've missed the ferry, darling,' he wheezes down the line. 'I'm afraid we're going to be late home.'

'Missed the ferry?' I parrot. 'How did you manage that when Mother's usually shit-the-bed early for everything?!'

'We got our collars felt at the port,' he mumbles, audibly cringing.

'Eh? What for?' I almost choke.

'Smuggling tobacco.'

'What the...?'

'Listen, it was all your Mother's doing,' he tells me in an inadequately low voice.

'Oh, you are a cruel man, Desmond!' comes her voice in the background. 'If exaggeration were a sport, you'd be an Olympic gold medallist!'

'Well, it all stems back to that bloody video channel of yours, doesn't it?' he yells. 'If you hadn't started all that stuff and nonsense with Gerald, then there would've been no need to promise him the world in duty-free cigars! Not that he deserves them, of course, after that rotten stunt he pulled with the channel name.'

I cover my ears, wondering how long this is all going to take.

'Anyhow, that's by the by now,' he exclaims, clearing his throat.

'Well, what on earth happened then?' I ask.

He takes a deep breath. 'Your Mother, in her infinite wisdom, thought she was doing Uncle Gerald a great service buying as many cigars as she could. Then we get to the checkpoint and see that the limit's only fifty cigars and we've got two hundred of the bloody things! So we had to hide as many as we could. We had them hidden under the seats, under the spare wheel, in the waistband of your mother's bloody skirt, even! There I am, sweating like molten iron and she's sat cool as a cucumber; reckoned we wouldn't get stopped because we look well-heeled. Only, they *did* stop us and they found the bloody lot in all of thirty seconds! Well, that was it. We were hauled out the car. Had to have our fingerprints done, pictures taken, the lot!' he explains.

Unable to hold it any longer, I burst into fits of laughter just picturing the unlikely scene.

'It's not funny, love. I thought we were going

to be locked up!' he gasps.

Well, it wouldn't be the first time where Mother's concerned!

'Listen, Dad, Dan and I have an appointment at the bank at 4 pm for mortgage advice. It's been booked for ages,' I explain. 'Dan's working through part of his lunch break so he can get away early to meet me there and I've organised for Sharon to have the twins, but what am I going to do with the dog? I can't leave him alone in the flat. He'll wreck the place! He wrecks it when I'm there with him!'

'Oh!' he exclaims. 'Well, could Sharon not mind him at theirs while you're at the bank?'

'Not unless you want him set upon by a Great Dane!' I reply.

He pauses briefly, as though weighing up the idea.

'Dad?'

'Er, yes, I'm still here, love,' he mumbles. 'Leave it with me. I'm fairly sure I can think of someone who owes us a favour!'

My phone buzzes a few minutes after Dad has hung up.

Dad: *Uncle Gerald coming for dog at 2 pm. Make sure you take him to toilet! Dad x*

Ping!

Dad: *Take dog, I mean. Not Uncle Gerald! x*

I send Sharon off with Mia and Jack at the pre-arranged time of 1.30 pm. As suspected, 2 pm comes and goes with no sign of Uncle Gerald. Knew it! It had all seemed way too easy and convenient. Why did Dad think we could rely on that useless great jerkoff?! Where is he?! Surely Dad told him I have things to do and places to be?

By 2.30 pm I'm in a state of panic. My bus comes in less than fifteen minutes. If Uncle Gerald and his pompous arse do not arrive imminently, I'm going to miss Dan at the bank and we'll have yet another row adding yet *more* cracks to our marriage and giving him yet *more* excuses to justify running off with Amber bloody Ross!

'Right, move it, mutt!' I growl, deciding to wait out on the street so that the moment Uncle Gerald draws up – assuming he actually will – I can dump the dog on him, make like a guillotine and head off sharpish!

As luck would have it, Horatio decides to foul the pavement just as, at 2.36 pm, a large silver estate draws up with Uncle Gerald crammed behind the wheel looking rather bent of out shape.

Uncle Gerald scowls through the driver window, moustache twitching irritably. 'Stick the damn thing in the back.'

Retching, I grab a doggy bag from my coat pocket, begrudgingly pick up Horatio's farewell present, and tie the handles. With no time to lose, I toss the bag onto the back seat, sending Uncle Gerald into a fit of rage.

'Not that! The dog, you ignoramus!' he roars from the front with a face like a big, angry cherry.

'S-sorry,' I mutter, fishing the bag out and sticking it in my coat pocket for now as I grapple to get the dog inside.

'Get a wiggle on, girl. I've got things to do!' he badgers, as I glare at the back of his fat grey head, battling the urge to punch it.

Grrr! If I were a bird, I know who'd I'd shit on!

Seething, I bundle the dog inside the car and quickly slam the door, watching from the pavement and smiling triumphantly as the car pulls off sharply and the back of Horatio's barking head disappears off down the street.

'Good luck, mate! You're gonna need it,' I mutter, sprinting off to the bus stop.

Glancing at my watch, I make it 2.39 pm. Cool! The bus isn't due till 2.45 pm. *I'm doing better for time than I thought,* I think to myself, popping into the newsagents for a drink.

What should've been a near enough instant purchase turns into a lengthy wait as the old dear paying for her Woman's Weekly in front counts out £1.50 in coppers. I peer over her shoulder into her purse rammed with silver and pound coins.

Bugger me, what is it with old people and their compelling need to get rid of change?

I watch as the bus chugs up outside, causing my stomach to drop. Fuck!

'Sorry, my bus is here. I've got a Dr Pepper, can I leave the money on the counter?' I ask the shopkeeper, to which he gives a stern nod. 'Thanks-keep-the-change,' I blurt, tripping over the wheel of the old dear's shopping trolley in my hurry to leave, Dr Pepper dropping out my hands in the process. Flustered, I grab it from the floor and bolt out the door at a rate of knots.

The bus doors clatter shut just as I reach them, forcing me to bang them down like those people who always hold the bus up, the ones you sit giving daggers to from the comfort of your seat, secretly hoping the driver drives off without them.

Luckily, he lets me on.

Mental note: *Must try to acquire bus driver-like sympathy and patience going forward.*

Once the psychic inkling between my shoulders tells me that the other passengers have stopped staring, I settle back into my seat and unscrew my drink ... which loudly fizzes up and sprays me full frontal! Face contorted in horror and psychic inkling making a swift return, I can't get the bottle done up fast enough!

Great. Just what you need right before an appointment to discuss grown up and mature things such as buying houses.

Puffing and panting, I burst into the bank ten minutes late. I spot Dan sat in a tub chair in the waiting area, looking painedly at his watch from under his sexy, David Beckham-esque furrowed brows.

He sighs. 'I wasn't sure if you were coming,' he says, rising out of his seat on my approach. 'Where've you been?'

'I'll tell you later, it's too long a story,' I pant, still catching my breath.

He rolls his eyes and makes that huffing sound he always does when he assumes off the bat that everything's *my* fault. Beckham brows or not, I'm counting that as another sign of his contempt for me, the jilted wife.

'I didn't realise it was raining out,' he remarks, straining to look out of the windows at the entrance to the bank.

'Sorry?'

'I said I didn't know it was raining,' he repeats, gesturing toward my mad hair, still wet from the Dr Pepper volcano.

'Oh. It's not,' I mutter, leaving him scratching his head just as a lofty guy with salt and pepper hair appears from a side room and gestures for us to follow him.

'Good afternoon to the both of you, I'm Shaun,' he greets us in a polished voice, stepping forward to shake our hands when we're in the room. 'Oh, is it raining out there?' he frowns, staring at my hair.

'Um,' I murmur, looking to Dan who shoots me a strange look. 'A little bit,' I smile, quickly shaking his hand and taking a seat.

'Right, so you're here for some mortgage advice.' He smiles. 'Is it your first property that you're looking to buy, or do you own currently?'

'We're first-time buyers,' Dan reveals.

Nodding, Shaun launches into a long-winded spiel about the housing market and interest rates, none of which I understand or am even taking in as I sit scanning Dan's shirt collar for lipstick marks.

'So, for a three-bed semi in this area you could be looking at anything from two right up to eight hundred thousand, budget depending,' he announces. 'And what sort of term would you be wanting?' he asks, turning his attention toward me.

'Term?' I parrot back at him, clueless.

He smiles. 'Yes, the term in which you'd like to repay the mortgage.'

'Dunno. A few years?' I suggest, wondering if

it's a trick question.

Dan quickly cuts in with a number umpteen times greater, leaving me squirming, fanning my burning face and praying Shaun directs all questions to the hubby henceforth.

As they continue with the number crunching, I notice an unpleasant, periodic whiff emanating from somewhere as yet unknown. I sniff the air discreetly, nostrils flared with a repulsed grimace. Eww! What is it?

My first thought is to check the soles of my shoes under the table. Finding them to be surprisingly clean, I assess the following possible causes:

> 1. *Dan or mortgage adviser's breath.*
>
> 2. *Dan or mortgage adviser has stood in shit.*
>
> 3. *Dan or mortgage adviser has sharted.*

I go on to rule Dan out from numbers one and three, since he never has bad breath and, to date, I've never heard him fart, so it seems pretty unlikely that he'd pop one out in the bank of all places. Plus he came straight from work. What are the chances that he's trodden in shit in the very short distance from the car park? Dan's not the type of person to tread in shit. He's way too sexy. No, that rules out number two.

It's got to be the mortgage adviser, I think to myself, staring at him accusingly with narrowed eyes.

Five minutes on, the smell has quickly advanced from an unpleasant periodic whiff to fully established stench, so much so that I keep catching Dan turning and looking at me contemptuously every now and then. This is possibly another clue to his infidelity to add to the fast-growing list, but it's probably more likely that he assumes the smell is emanating from my direction. Damn cheek!

The mortgage adviser stops writing on the notepad in front of him, reaches over to the fan on his desk and switches it on, which only has the effect of circulating the smell throughout this small-scale side room all the more! With the three of us sat rigid in our chairs and the mortgage adviser now visibly gagging, I conclude that the stench can't be him after all and proceed to re-check my shoes. As I see for the second time that they're clean, I recall the day's events and, subsequently, Horatio's shit still buried in my coat pocket.

Fuck.

FUCK!

I leap up from my chair. 'Um, would you excuse me please? I just remembered, I have a … a…' I trail off as they both stare at me expectantly. 'Smear test!' I blurt, uttering the first thing that springs to mind.

Turning on my heel, I flee the bank and

scurry to the nearest bin on the street. I toss the offending item inside and momentarily debate jumping in there myself for a little respite from the big, bad world which, for some reason, seems to always be out to get me.

Chapter 14:

Bibbidi-Bobbidi-Poo!

At the end of every Christmas, I tell myself I'll be slim for the next one. Then, before I can say Terry's Chocolate Orange, the next Christmas is here and I'm heavier than the bloody last! Well, apart from the one year I spent in America, eating what amounted to rabbit food Monday to Friday … and look how long that lasted!

I guess that's what happens when you spend fifty-two weeks of the year telling yourself that the diet starts Monday. I suppose it's all down to priorities, and in a battle between being thin and eating chocolate, chocolate wins the day. Personally, I blame the food manufacturers. It's a well-known fact that unhealthy food is made to be addictive so that people buy more and more of it. I mean, nobody's growing carrots to be irresistible, are they? No. It simply goes without saying that anything with a high fat content is profoundly lush! What a shame that the same formula doesn't apply to actual people.

Then there's the supermarkets working against you. I once read that they deliberately waft that yummy smell of baked fare around the store on purpose to entice shoppers to the bakery section. Bastards! Still, I suppose they can't very well do the same with vegetables, can they? No. The store would smell like one giant fart!

At the end of the day, you can't eat like Henry Tudor all year and expect to have the figure of a ballet dancer come December. Science just doesn't work like that.

God, I hate science!

Having not long given birth to twins, I really can't be worrying about it … at least not until the first Monday in January, anyway. But when Dan arrives home from work the first week in December waving around a formal-looking gold envelope, suddenly I'm beyond worried.

'We have our invitation to this year's Christmas work do, babe!' he chirps. 'It's on the 18th. They've gone all-out! It's a five-course dinner-dance at a five-star luxury golf hotel.'

Suddenly, Carl Orff's "Carmina Burana" crashes through my head at ninety-thousand decibels! Holy flaps! And there was me thinking the only thing I need be concerning myself with this Christmas is whether to make breakfast on Christmas morning or just delve straight into the chocolate … yeesh!

Dan shoots me a strange look. 'Lizzie, you look like you're about to throw up!'

'Err, I think I … left the oven on!' I lie, careering through to the kitchen at speed and steadying myself on the countertop while scary visions of me looking overfed and underdressed in five-star surroundings near enough cripple me with anxiety. Oh, fuck. Fuuuuuuck! I've nothing to wear! I am literally Cinderella, only without the massive doe eyes, button nose, perfect teeth and dainty little figure. In fact, I can't think of a single Disney princess attribute I have in common with Cinderella, except that neither of us seem to leave the house!

I cannot possibly go. Well, not unless my Fairy Godmother bursts out from the cleaning cupboard right this second, waves her magic wand and bibbidi-bobbidi-boos me into Charlize Theron! Sadly, the only thing in the cleaning cupboard is a manky mop, possibly still damp from that effing flood. Hmph! Even the mop would probably scrub up for a five-course dinner-dance better than I could … perhaps Dan would be better taking that as his plus-one?

Having spent the entire night tossing and turning, then waking from a nightmare in which I was stark naked at Dan's work's Christmas do, grappling furiously to cover everything with only my hands when it would've taken several pairs, it's little wonder I'm struggling through the next day on the backfoot, bleary-eyed and zombie-like.

'Cooey! Elizabeth? Elizabeth, are you there?' come Mother's infuriating shrill from the answer machine that afternoon.

Damn, I must have nodded off and missed the phone!

'Oh, *do* hurry up and pick up!'

Ugh! Why does she do that? *Why?!* I mean, why doesn't it ever occur to her that I might be out instead of just assuming I'm at home and hiding from the phone?! Although, to be fair, I *am* home and I *often* hide from the phone ... but still!

'Now, I'm just calling to remind you about my annual festive soirée, dear. It's scheduled for the last Saturday before Christmas, that is to say the 18th, dear,' she goes on.

I freeze on my way over to the landline, my weary scowl now but a ghost as I listen on in intrigue.

The 18th, she says. That's the same night as the dinner-dance!

Suddenly, I'm all ears.

'Now, it's very important that you come, dear. I've a lot of ground to make up for since the...' she trails off with a slight gulp, '*incident* at my last function. So, I've invited the local MP. He's awfully nice! Verrry handsome! And he's a real family-man so it's important that I have *my* family around *me*, dear, so I can show him that he's amongst his own.'

Charming!

'It'll be the usual thing, dear. Carols and canapes with some tasteful party games. I'll make up the bed in the spare room so you can stay over. Looking forward to it!'

Click. She's gone.

Damn. Two invitations to Christmas parties on the same night – although, to be fair, Mother's is more a summons than an invitation. Hm, now let me think, Mother or Margot? Which is worse? Well, usually the anti-climax of one of Mother's festive soirées is on a similar level to receiving a lump of coal in one's stocking, but if it means me getting out of having to meet Dan's colleagues at a time when my body confidence is lower than a snake's midriff, then I'm game!

Later...

'You what? Let the team down just to attend another of your Mum's poncey soirées?' Dan very nearly chokes over dinner. 'Not going to happen, Lizzie.'

'Oh, so it's work before family now, is it?' I glare across the table.

Or is the thought of an evening spent with me and not Amber too much to bear?

'Well, *you've* changed your tune! Last year you said you'd rather stick a piece of steak to your tits and run through a pack of starving dogs than go to another of your Mum's Christmas get-togethers,' he points out under raised brows.

I give a shady sideward glance. 'Well … well, even so, she's family, isn't she?' I argue feebly.

Dan slams down his fork with a sigh. 'Work's invite came first. I'm still a newbie and team-playing's a big part of the job role. I need to fit in. I'm *going*, Lizzie. I really hoped it would've been with my wife by my side, but hey, if you'd rather stand there being insulted by your Uncle Gerald all night, then it's your call.'

'You mean you'd go without me?' I challenge, already consumed by FOMO.

He shrugs. 'Well, yeah. If I have to.'

Inner twat: *Dan and Margot up the tree, K-I-S-S-I-N-G!*

His look softens, possibly due to my Tiny Tim-esque expression. 'Listen, my probation period is up soon and then we'll be able to apply for that mortgage, babe.' He smiles, placing his hand over mine and giving it a squeeze. 'Just tell your mum we already have plans. I'll ask my folks to have the twins for the weekend and we'll get to spend some quality time together.'

I give a tepid nod, totally lit at the idea of spending time with the man I love at Christmas, but worried shitless about making a good impression … something I've always been extraordinarily bad at.

∞∞∞

'Are you nuts? Nobody in their right mind would turn down a free five-course dinner-dance at a five-star hotel at Christmas!' Becca gasps over coffee at the community centre later in the week.

'Yes, but…' I trail off. 'Well, *look* at me!'

She shrugs, wide-eyed. 'I'm looking.'

'I can't go, Becca. They're all attractive, intelligent executives and I'm a frumpy housewife with all the class and decorum of … of … well, I don't know, one those monkeys you see at the zoo with their arses out. I honestly have nothing to wear and—'

'Lizzie, you're bonkers if you don't go!' Becca snorts, shaking her head in disbelief.

'Listen, Becca. When I tell you I have absolutely nothing to wear, I actually mean I have absolutely nothing to wear!' I protest, hoping my stern, rhythmic nods allude to the severity of the situation while I simultaneously try to forget all of the lovely size eight dresses I used to be able to wear in what now seems like another life.

Becca rolls her eyes back at me, totally unconvinced. 'Lizzie, the shops are crammed with glitzy party wear this time of year. We're no longer in the Dark Ages – most of them cater for plus-size these days. It's really not a big deal.'

I pause for a moment, face falling as visions of me sweating, swearing and struggling into various spangly tents in changing rooms across London begin charging at me from all angles.

Shit, I feel knackered just thinking about it!

'Nobody's perfect! It's about making the best of what you have to work with. Finding a look that plays up your best parts and being the best version of yourself,' Becca goes on.

A hopeful half-smile etches its way up my face while a scene reminiscent of an old Hollywood movie plays out in my mind…

A black cab drawing up outside a magnificent countryside venue trussed with twinkling lights. The passenger door opening as I step out into the evening air in an uber-sophisticated, shimmering spaghetti-strap dress. Passersby stopping and turning to look, bedazzled by my elegance and my alluring smile. A dapper Dan walking from around the other side of the cab, taking my hand and leading me proudly up the rustic stone steps to the grand open entrance doors, the approving glint in his eye telling me that all-night lovemaking is definitely on the cards later! Hm.

Trouble is, in this vision of mine, I'm skinny as fuck, my arse is tiny and I actually have a waist again! I'm not just the best version of myself, I'm a totally different effing person! Realistically, I'll probably fall out of the cab head-first, crying and late.

'Look, Lizzie, it's Christmas! Go and enjoy yourself! Eat, drink and be merry! That's truly what it's all about,' Becca soothes, taking a long sip of her abandoned coffee and pulling a face when she finds it cold. In normal circumstances she'd be right and I'd be soothed, but there's one majorly troubling thing getting in the way of all that: Amber ruddy Ross!

Inner twat: *She'll be all glowing and mesmeric. Dan will notice and spend the rest of his life asking why the fuck he married Lizzie Bradshaw, total degenerate and ARSE!*

Inner voice of reason: *She'll be taking a plus-one and, even if she isn't, she's management and thus will be sat on a table with all the other managers, most likely on the opposite side of the room far, far away, offering ample opportunity for relaxed merry-making.*

With this in mind, later on that afternoon I embark upon the unthinkable: phoning Mother to decline her invite.

'Well, can't Daniel ask them to have their

Christmas party some other night instead?' she barks down the line post-bombshell.

'I can't honestly see them going for that,' I murmur, wondering if she actually believes a large limited company would base its plans around the wants and needs of one man's haughty mother-in-law.

'Oh, but it's such a shame, dear! Of all the nights for them to have a Christmas party and they go and choose *my* Christmas party night!' she complains with the sort of vitriol usually reserved for Delia Davenport.

'Hm, sod's law, isn't it?' I lie, having decided that attending the same event as Dan's movie star boss sure beats being sprayed with pork pie by Uncle Gerald as he combines wolfing finger foods with berating me publicly.

'Well, why don't I give them a call to explain —'

'Fuck no!' I screech down the line in panic.

'Good grief, Elizabeth! Must you use language of the gutter?'

'Well, you see, this job is the best thing to happen to Dan,' I say, ravishing boss aside, of course. 'We're only a few weeks off being able to apply for our mortgage, so he needs to keep his nose clean and stay in favour with them. He'd be mortified if you called them. Oh, promise me you won't!'

Silence, for once.

'Mother, promise you won't call them!' I demand.

'It's okay, Elizabeth. You go off and enjoy your festive dinner-dance and don't give it another thought,' she replies breezily.

Wait, she's being reasonable?

'Tomorrow isn't promised to any of us. I mean, who knows if I'll even be around this time next year to put on another of my festive soirées? This year could very well be the last. But, of course, work comes before family, dear.'

No, she's being a tit!

Beep, beep, beep … she's gone!

∞∞∞

It's Friday 17th and I still haven't found anything to wear to the dinner-dance tomorrow night. While cutting it fine has been a life-long forte, it seems everything has been working against my best efforts to find an outfit. It's almost a foregone conclusion that anything half-decent is well out of my price range, and with Christmas now just a week away I can't justify spending silly money on something I likely won't wear again. I mean, how often do Dan and I go to five-star venues?

As the high street winds down and door shutters *click-clack* to a close around me, I flag down a black cab and venture home pissed off, empty-handed and feet killing!

With the twins packed off to Rob and Sharon's for the weekend, this was the perfect chance for Dan and me to spend a cosy, Christmassy couple of days together. Any normal, organised person would have had their outfit hanging in the wardrobe ready to go weeks ago and be snuggled up on the sofa watching films in the ambiance of the Christmas tree lights, sipping Baileys and Eggnog. Okay, maybe not Eggnog, but still I should be full of festive spirit right now, and I'm not. Instead, I have that foul, impending sense of doom ... the one that tells you everything's about to go spectacularly tits up!

'You're up early! Where are you off to?' Dan remarks, appearing in the front room in just his boxers the next morning, as I stand grappling with the buttons on my coat by the front door.

'I've, er, just got to get some bits for tonight,' I mumble, stopping short of telling him "bits" actually means "an entire effing outfit"!

'Please tell me you've got something to wear,' he says with a weary sigh.

'Yes. Yes, of course! What do you take me for?' I ask indignantly, as though I'm not about to run laps around the mall re-assessing everything I browsed yesterday in hopes that, as if by magic, it's suddenly wearable. Or, better yet, that some glam new lines have arrived in store only this morning, all expertly skimming the Mr Greedy belly, slimming down the ham arms, and basically making me look a size ten at a bargain price.

A girl can dream!

Glancing at my watch in the middle of the manic, jam-packed shopping mall, my throat begins to close up and I go all hot as I realise I have just one hour left to source the perfect outfit for tonight or I am going to be seriously in the shit! I know exactly what it is I need, but as time goes on I'm starting to think that what I need might only exist in my own head and is yet to actually be made.

Then, just as I begin scurrying out of the umpteenth clothes store with my heart in my mouth, I see it…

A wine-coloured, sparkly, floaty chiffon belted tunic with a Bardot neckline, long enough to cover my belly and with long, fluted sleeves to keep the old bingo wings under wraps. It's glamorous, it's festive, it's affordable … it's perfect! Oh, but let me guess, they don't have it in my size? No, wait. They do! They actually do!

Feeling like all my Christmases have come at once, I snatch it from the rail and clutch it protectively to my chest as though it were as precious one of my children – let's face it, right now it probably is! In a lightbulb moment, my entire look comes together: sparkly wine-coloured tunic, sophisticated black wide-leg trousers (obviously with elasticated waistband for post-five-course meal comfort), black satin high heeled mules, blingy bracelet, silver clutch, chandelier earrings, loose waves pinned to the side with high-fashion quiff, matching wine-coloured lips, fingers and toes, with shimmering eyes and candlelit complexion.

Hm. Can see me struggling with the last two, but what the hell?! I have my outfit ... Cinders *shall* go to the ball!

Later...

Shower-fresh and hair in giant turban, I stand rifling through the drawers in the bedroom. Tonight is *definitely* the occasion to wear my best bra – a black lace Gossard plunge that gives unbeatable lift and separation! Hm, but on second thoughts, the neckline on my tunic is pretty risqué. Would wearing the Gossard be over-egging the pudding?

'Well, it's a five-star establishment. Totally not the sort of place one walks around with their baps out,' I mumble to myself, reaching for a minimiser instead.

Next, something to minimise my behind. Pulling open my knicker drawer, I select a pair of black, firm control shaper shorts, quite forgetting that it's a five-course meal and so not really the occasion to be sat rigid in a torniquet of spandex. Fuck, me! They're way smaller than I remember. I can barely get them past my knees! Cursing and flustered, I spend the next few minutes grappling with them. By hook or by crook, I *will* get my arse into these shaper shorts!

'Oh, just get *on* you utter, utter bastards!' I grimace, smashing full pelt into the bedroom door.

'Lizzie? Lizzie, are you okay?' comes Dan's voice from outside seconds later.

'Don't come in! Do not come in!' I roar in response, fearful that this highly compromising position I'm in currently could very well initiate the end of our sex life- forevermore!

'Sorry for caring,' he mumbles, his footsteps disappearing off down the hall.

Deciding that comfort beats a shapely arse hands-down anyway, I toss the shaper shorts across the room in fury and select a pair of my largest passion killers. Yes, I'm only in my early thirties, but nothing, and I mean *nothing*, beats big pants for comfort!

Next, I pull on my sophisticated, black wide-leg trousers. *Skimming and classy*, I decide, turning this way and that in the wardrobe mirror and perfectly ignoring its cries that I look pregnant and it's either Ben or Jerry's!

Smiling, I reach for my lifesaving sparkly, wine-coloured floaty chiffon tunic, which, for some reason I'm having difficulty getting over my head. Wait … what?!

As I stand examining it, open-mouthed, it quickly dawns upon me that my lifesaving, sparkly, wine-coloured floaty chiffon tunic is, in actual fact, a playsuit … a very *short* playsuit! And there was me worried about over-egging the pudding! Pfft! Never mind over-egging the pudding, the pudding's fucked! How in the hell did I fail to spot those effing leg holes? It looked like a tunic! It *still* looks like a bloody tunic, even as I stand here staring at it, willing said leg holes to piss off!

'Lizzie, what on earth's going on in there?!' comes Dan's voice at the door again.

'Nothing! Just … just go away, would you?!' I yell back in a super-stressy voice that tells him all is definitely *not* good in the hood.

'Listen, whatever's going on we have less than an hour before the taxi arrives and I need to get into the bedroom to dress,' he warns.

'AlrightI'llbeoutsoon!' I bawl in one screechy syllable, flinging open the wardrobe door. A small part of me contemplates getting in it and pissing off to Narnia.

Fuck! This can't be! This cannot bloody well be!

Voice in head: *Well, you never know, it might actually look okay on.*

Voice of reason: *Don't be a dick!*

In a total non-brainwave, I whip off the trousers, put on the playsuit and try the trousers over it. I look in the mirror. It's no good. The playsuit just adds even more bulk underneath and, with a waistline about as defined as The Snowman's, I look like Humpty-bleeding-Dumpty!

With the clock ticking, I reach for the only possible option: the ditsy floral wrap dress. Only, I can't see it hanging anywhere. Fuck. After angrily pulling out the entire side of my wardrobe onto the bedroom floor, I find it screwed up into a ball, creased to high heaven and unwashed in my overnight bag from Rob's sixtieth. Oh, why can't I be more like Martha Stewart goddammit?!

'Lizzie, I need to come in and get dressed,' Dan badgers from outside the door five minutes later.

'Ugh, alright!' I snap.

'Oh,' he remarks in surprise, freezing partway through the now open door. 'Is that what you're wearing?'

I peer down at my patterned peplum top paired with the black wide-leg trousers. 'Why, what's the matter with it?'

'Nothing. I just, er, assumed you'd be wearing a dress,' he replies.

I pause in place by the wardrobe. 'Should I get changed, then?!' I huff, hands-on-hips.

'No! There's no time, Lizzie. You've been pissing about for too long already,' Dan snaps, storming over to his side of the wardrobe and yanking out his suit.

He shouted at me. And he said a swear! Two more pointers to his infidelity!

'Oh. Well, I'm sorry that I'm not good enough for you,' I mutter through pursed lips, grabbing my make-up bag off the dressing table and retreating to the bathroom in a rage.

'Don't be ridiculous!' he sighs waspishly on my way out.

Less than half an hour later, if the beleaguered panda looking back at me in the bathroom mirror is anything to go by, I think we can safely say that the shimmering eyes and candlelit complexion hasn't happened. Alas, nor have the loose waves with high-fashion quiff, and the less we say about my fingers and toes the better.

'Taxi's here!' Dan shouts from the front

room, sending a super-charged bolt of anxiety careering through my central nervous system. Of all the words in the world, *those* are the two a woman least wants to hear when she's not ready and nothing's going in accordance with the red carpet-like visions she'd had of her looking her absolute, radiant best.

'But my hair's not done!' I yell back at him, panic rising.

'The meter's running, you've no time for that now!' he counters, his tone highly indicative that if I'm not out of the bathroom in ten seconds, he's going to carry me out kicking and screaming in a fireman's lift. Ok, possibly a little ambitious with my weight.

Well, that's it then! With the distinct absence of any Fairy Godmother to get me out of this one, it looks like Cinders is pretty fucked.

Chapter 15:

A Christmas Cracker

After a mostly silent journey following a heated row about my 'always making us late', the cab turns off into a long, wooded entrance lit by tall lanterns dressed with plush, red velvet bows. Already I can tell the place is something else and, as we turn the corner, the full splendour of the stately English manor, exquisitely embellished with soft, gold twinkling lights, is revealed at the bottom of a long driveway flanked by tall pines. I could almost be in a Christmas film. Under normal circumstances, I'd probably be pretending that I *am*, but with all the Christmas spirit of Ebeneezer Scrooge between us, I guess it's going to be another item on a growing list of wasted occasions.

As we draw up outside the entrance, Dan leans across to pay the driver. Despite us not talking, he *still* walks around the cab to open my door for me. I smile up at him awkwardly, draw in a deep breath, and climb out, every bit as overfed and underdressed as I'd envisaged.

'This way,' he mutters.

My face drops as he strolls off out in front toward the open entrance doors, leaving me tottering behind. I had hoped he'd hold my hand – not just because I can't walk so well in these bastard shoes, but because, now more than ever, I need one of his reassuring squeezes.

'Good evening, sir,' a waiter smiles from inside the foyer, handing Dan a glass of champagne from a well-stocked, ornate silver tray as he ventures inside.

Voice in head: *Alcohol! Thank fuck!*

'Madam.' He nods, offering the tray out toward me.

I grab and neck a glass in what is near enough a single gulp, acquiring myself a distinctly appalled look.

'Er, can I take your glass, madam?' he enquiries.

'Oh! Thanks.' I giggle nervously, placing it down on the tray and hurrying off to catch up with Dan who is already stood chatting with some younger guy who looks like he's walked straight off the set of *Made in Chelsea*.

'Oh, er, Julian, this is my wife, Lizzie,' Dan announces when I reach his side. 'Lizzie, this is Julian, one of the salesmen in our team.'

'*Best* salesman, I would add!' he scoffs, his

voice laden with enough braggadocio to tell me he's an arse. 'Call me Ju,' he winks, as though it's that much cooler.

I nod, offering out my hand. He shakes it limply, looking me up and down with an unfriendly smirk, as though he might gain five stone just from shaking my hand.

Voice in head: *Well, he can swivel if he thinks I'm going to call him Ju now. As of this moment, I'm nicknaming him Ju-drop.*

'Er, shall we head into the bar?' Dan cuts in after a tense pause, leading the way as I dither behind like a lost sheep. I'm consumed by that "first day at school" feeling, where you don't know what to do or where to place yourself. I can almost hear the distant echo of Mother's voice reprimanding me for fidgeting and telling me how lower-class it is.

As we enter the bustling reception bar, I spot *her* almost instantly. She's standing goddess-like to my left, wearing a classy gold evening gown and enthralling and captivating the small crowd that have gathered around and are hanging off her every word. Everything seems to move in slow motion while I observe her blonde, tousled bob bouncing off her slender, tanned shoulders as she laughs. Her striking green eyes dance and her Hollywood smile dazzles.

She: *The fairy on top of the Christmas tree.*

Me: *The pig in blanket.*

Suddenly I feel as irrelevant as Slade on Boxing Day and, as I catch sight of my reflection in the holly-draped mirror opposite, it would appear that mad hair is something else I have in common with Noddy Holder tonight. And as for that candlelit complexion? Well, let's just say it's looking less candlelight and more Tin Man from *The Wizard of Oz*. Oh for God's sake, it's as though everything that could have gone wrong has, and we've barely set foot in the bloody building!

Dan's voice from over at the bar brings me out of my trance and back down to earth. 'Lizzie, what do you want to drink?' he asks, waving his hand around to get my attention as Ju-drop continues to look me up and down.

'Oh, er…' I look around at the shelves of alcohol behind the barman.

'Um, can I get a Jack—'

His face falls dramatically before he gives me that *please don't get pissed* look I've come to know and hate.

'Alright, a gin and lemonade,' I say relentingly.

He nods, and I stand watching in despair as my single 25ml shot of Dutch courage is cancelled-out by a monsoon of lemonade!

As I stand engulfed in the heat of the many

stares fixed upon me, I totally get why people like Uncle Tony might find comfort and solace at the bottom of a whisky bottle. Human beings can be so rude and judgemental! Even when they know that you know they're looking, they carry on staring, assessing, scrutinising. I can almost hear their thoughts of 'Who the fuck invited *that*?!'

'Is that 007 or my best sales exec?' comes a sultry voice to my side, followed by wildly exaggerated laughter.

'Oh, Amber!' Dan laughs bashfully, spinning around and fixing his still-perfect hair. Ju-drop follows suit, running his hands through his over-oiled combover. 'You're looking lovely this evening,' Dan says with an appraising smile.

He didn't say that to me, and I'm his wife! But then again, I do look like I got dressed in the dark…

Amber leans across for the executive double cheek kiss and I see Dan's brief downward eye-dip confirming he's noticed her pert and glistening little cleavage. I glance down at my own – a straight line of granny-tit spanning from my sternum nearly all the way up to my chin – and conclude I should have worn the Gossard for that unbeatable lift and separation, even if it does nearly slice me in two.

'And look at *you*, you dapper thing!' she grins, playfully brushing the arm of his suit.

'Oh, stop! You're making me blush!' He

laughs, pulling a silly face as mine crumples beside him. 'Oh, er, Amber, I'd like you to meet my other half, Lizzie' he quickly adds.

'Hello,' I greet her in a fraudulent chirp, peering out from around his side.

'Oh? I thought you were on your ownsome tonight?' she remarks, not even looking in my direction.

Rude!

'Hello,' I repeat with decidedly less chirp.

Finally, she acknowledges me. '*Oh*! Hello!' she gasps, hand clasped to clavicle. 'I didn't see you sat there. Don't get up.'

Don't get up? I'm bloody stood already!

Demeaned, I step out from beside Dan into full view, prompting her perfect face to fall. 'Oh, I'm so sorry! You looked as though you were sitting down.' She giggles awkwardly and playfully whacks Dan's arm. 'It's *your* fault. You're so tall, everybody looks short next to you!'

Oh, get a bloody room!

'Well, I'd best go and mingle then,' she adds through a bewitching smile. 'Oh and, er, lovely to meet you, Lydia,' she adds half-heartedly over her shoulder.

'Well. *She* seems nice,' I mutter.

Or not. And totally not the professional busi-

nesswoman I had her down for. She obviously fancies him. I knew it! I bloody well knew it!

'Yeah, she's great.' Dan smiles, before turning his attention back to Ju-drop who launches into a rigmarole of self-praise for all the sales commission he bagged last month.

A little before 7.30 pm, the congregation in the bar begins to disperse as people filter off into the ballroom for dinner. We follow suit, making our way into a most spectacular setting dressed with lit trees, garlands and red poinsettias. The festive ambiance is rounded off by a pianist playing Christmas songs on a grand piano, and there's an air of excitement among the executive, over-confident voices coming at me from all directions as each of us scour the place cards on the impeccably set tables.

'Dan!' comes *that* voice. 'Dan, over here! You're with us!'

I turn to see a beaming Amber waving wildly and patting the single, vacant seat beside her. Glowering, I crane my neck toward the chair at the other side of her to observe its occupant as some trendy, middle-aged woman with a bright red, blunt-cut bob, whom I think it's fair to say is definitely not Amber's plus-one.

Rat's bollocks. She's single!

'I think you moight be next to me, bab,' comes a male Brummie accent over on the opposite side of the table.

Oh. Sticking me as far away from her and Dan as possible so she can sit and flirt her perky little tits off with him all night. I see!

I look to Dan who, to be fair, looks just as surprised as I do, but say nothing and make my way over to the old bloke with three chins. Oh, spiffing. Bloody spiffing! I mean, what am I going to talk about with this man all night long? Chins aside, we have zero in common and I don't know him from a bar of bloody soap!

'Alroight, bab? I'm Frank.' He nods, his gaze slinking off down my top.

And he's a pervert ... how wonderful!

'Er, great, yes. Hello.'

I can already tell that I'm going to have to dig deep to find the kind of fortitude I'm not even sure I possess just to make it through the meal without making a scene. I haven't been this pissed off since McDonald's scrapped breakfast wraps! I mean, everybody knows how awkward these work gatherings are for plus-ones. What kind of a cruel bitch deliberately separates a couple and sticks the wife down the other end of the table on her tod? I swear if she dares say so much as a word to me for the rest of the night, my part of the conversation might just stretch to telling her to fuck off.

I draw in a deep, calm-inducing breath, my gaze resting upon the bountiful assortment of house wines displayed within dangerously easy reach, then back to Dan and Amber who are laughing and chatting away. My mental rendition of Brandy's "The Boy is Mine" begins drowning out the pianist.

An hour on…

'Hey! Hey! Doesn't it sound like "fucking pie" instead of "pumpkin pie"?!' I guffaw across the table, as Brenda Lee's "Rocking Around the Christmas Tree" rings out during the main course.

Silence … other than for my own roaring laughter, of course.

'Come on, you've all thought it too!' I snort in protest, giving minimal thought to the tirade of executive eyerolls I am met with from all corners of the table now that I've ever-so-slightly overdosed on the old Dutch courage. *Hicc!*

'Yeah, if you like,' scoffs some sarky schmuck in a snappy suit, triggering an array of muted sniggers.

I glance across the table in Dan's direction. He sits silently prodding his salad, lips pressed. Ah. I'm embarrassing him. Surely he didn't expect me to sit here on my tod with my head down, eating my meal and keeping myself to myself while he cavorts with *her* all night? Soulmates are meant to be sensitive to each other's feelings but here's Dan acting totally blind to mine this evening. This is a man whom, ordinarily, knows everything I'm thinking and feeling – sometimes before I even know myself – so surely he's aware that this is all a million miles out of my comfort zone? But could it be that he just doesn't care anymore?

'It dooes sound a bit loike fookin' pie, yer know,' Frank chuckles, coming to my defence two minutes too late.

Sigh.

'So! I hear you used to be in sales yourself, Lizzie,' the chap on the other side of Frank asks, leaning across the still-silent table to face me.

'Oh, yeah! *Yeah!* I used to hit all my KBI's,' I grin in a boastful slur, face falling as the bastards sit tittering into their turkey.

He frowns, puzzled. 'KBIs? That's an acronym for key business issues.'

Crap! Well, I definitely caused a shit tonne of those.

All eyes fall on me. I peer around the table, observing the huddle of mocking, arrogant faces staring back at me. Then I snap...

'Yes, well, I hated sales, anyway,' I retort louder than planned, vaguely aware of Dan's head shooting up across the table. 'Nothing's ever good enough! I mean, when you *do* actually hit your target, they just go and raise the bastard even higher!' I add in a pissed squeak. 'It's a mug's game. Totally unfulfilling. You're always chasing rainbows in sales.'

Silence.

'Bostin' grub, innit?' Frank cuts in awkwardly.

Somehow I make it to coffee and mints without punching anyone or being punched myself. Shit. This evening couldn't have gone any worse! What is it with me? I try my best, I really do. I'm polite to people, I put up with crappy treatment, and still they can't just be nice. *And if they are nice, they're too damn nice*, I think to myself, turning to observe Frank's chair which has been gradually inching closer and closer to me, such that if it moves any closer, he'll be on my fucking lap!

As well as conversing with my tits all night, Frank has an exhausting tendency to stop conversations and start totally new ones before he's even made his point. Every so often, he'll drop a pointless, random fact into the mix and, as he turns to face me, grinning his head off, I can tell another is imminent…

'Did yer know the largest ever human turd recorded in the history of mankoind was twenty centimetres in length and five centimetres in width?'

I grimace, mid-gulp of my coffee. 'Eww. Really?'

'Yeah, no shit!' he quips, roaring with laughter at the crap pun.

Frowning, I begin guesstimating 20cm by 5cm with my hands, acquiring some pretty odd looks from around the table. Granted, my estimates are probably going to be somewhat out. I mean, I've never been one for maths, pissed or not. Still, when I picture 20cm by 5cm in my mind, I can't see how that's a record.

'Are you sure that's right, Frank? It's certainly not what I'd call massive. I'm sure I've had bigger.'

The table falls silent.

'Oh!' I laugh. 'We weren't talking about Frank's penis, I can assure you!' I explain, deciding in what I can only put down to part nerves and part desperate need to win the stuffy bastards over that this could serve as a funny icebreaker. With my audience white-hot, I steal my opportunity. 'We were actually talking about turds,' I slur. 'Frank reckons the biggest ever recorded in the history of mankind came in at 20cm by 5cm and, I don't know about you, but I reckon I've definitely broken the record!' I laugh again, finding myself met with an array of disgusted faces rather than the shrieking belly laughs I'd anticipated.

Oh, crap. Not good. Not good at all. Look at that, not even a hint of a bloody smile! You wouldn't guess for a minute that these people enter the workroom via an effing great slide. Between them, they're about as fun as herpes! And oh God, Dan looks appalled. He's not touched me in weeks and he's not bloody likely to now he's informed about my record-breaking shits. Oh, fuck. FUCK! Why did I go and tell them something like that? Me and my mouth! Perhaps it would be safer to shut up and let Frank do the talking … providing it's not body talk, that is.

'Did yer know that a group of hippos is called a bloat?' Frank mumbles into my hair.

I shake my head lethargically.

'Yeah, tis, yer know.'

'Right.' I nod, not really grasping the point.

He leans in even closer as the rest of the table go back to their non-faeces related conversations. 'Bit loike us, innit?!'

'Sorry?'

'Me and you, bab!' He grins, patting down his Santa belly and nodding toward mine. 'We're in a bloat of our own!'

Me: *Right, that's it! The diet starts Monday!*

Also me: *It's Christmas next week! Chocolate for breakfast! Entire blocks of cheese! Pâté straight off the knife! The only time of year when it's acceptable* *to be pissed in your pyjamas three days in a row and anything goes!*

Me again: *And then after that it's winter. Hot drinks and hearty meals!*

Alas. There's just never a right time to lose fifty stone is there?

'Are you alroight, bab? Yer don't look very happy. What's oop wiv yer?' Frank remarks as the band begins warming up in the background.

After him basically calling me a hippo? Seriously?!

'Oh, nothing, I'm fine,' I lie through my teeth.

'Yer can't kid a kidder, loove,' he grunts with a knowing look. 'You've got a cob on about something.'

I shrug indifferently, glancing over toward Dan and his bae, still embroiled in conversation in their "secret club".

'Ah!' He chuckles, following my gaze. 'Well, you've noothin' ter be worried about there, bab,' he says, slapping my thigh in a way that I hope was meant to be reassuring.

Jesus. Surely it's past this old scrotum's nap time by now?

The band launches into their rendition of Mariah Carey's "All I Want for Christmas is You" and the dancefloor begins to fill.

'Fancy a dance?' Frank winks, offering out a giant, predatory hand.

I freeze in horror.

'Ah, coome on! Don't be a spoil sport!' he persists, as I frantically rack my brains for a bloody good excuse I can use.

'No, I'd better not. I've got a bad foot,' I say loudly over the music. It's not exactly ingenious but, well, I had to think on my feet – ingenious pun intended!

He shoots me a dubious look.

'No, honestly. The foot support is off now, but I really shouldn't push it,' I tell him in my best put-on serious tone.

He glances down at my feet and frowns. 'Well, what yer wearin' them stilts for then, bab? Are yer a glooton fer poonishment or soomfin?'

I peek down at my four-inch heels and give a slight gulp.

'You're not one of them toiypes that get aroused by pain, are yer?' he asks, a little too hopefully for my liking.

I slowly turn to face him in disbelief.

Minutes later, as the band bursts into Wham's "Last Christmas", I feel a tap on the shoulder. Oh, for God's sake, this is sexual harassment!

Why can't the git just take no for an answer?!

Fuming, I turn to see Dan stood at the back of my chair. My face lights up instantly.

'Do you want to dance?' he smiles, thumbing toward the dancefloor.

Voice in head: *He still loves me! He's forgiven me! Festive make-up sex!*

Before I can even open my mouth to talk, my newly unappointed Brummie minder waddles up to my side. 'She can't, fella. She's recooverin' from a foot injury, ain't yer, bab?' he shouts over the music.

Dan looks at me confused, totally not getting my desperate code faces.

And then from here, it all happens so quickly.

'Are you guys not dancing?' Amber enquiries, appearing suddenly at Dan's side.

'Lizzie's hurt her foot, apparently.' Dan shrugs.

'Ah, well, you'd better sit and have a rest then, hun. Frank will look after you, won't you, Frankie?' She beams.

'You can count on it,' he says with a nod and a seedy wink.

Oh, fuck!

'Come on then, Danny-boy! I'll be your dancing partner,' Amber says excitedly, pulling him off toward the dancefloor. I can only sit and watch, open-mouthed and broken-hearted, as they waltz under the glitterball to those iconic, melancholic, and now i-bloody-ronic verses. It's too close for comfort. Her body is closer to his than mine has been in weeks. The looks between them. The chemistry. Suddenly, it all makes sense: the leaving me on read, the coming home late all the time, his unusual tone-deaf behaviour. He's bloody in love with her!

I look on as time stands still. His right hand is rested upon the small of her back, her left gripping his shoulder as they sway in perfect synchrony to the music. And, you know what the saddest thing is? They look good together! She suits him in a way I never could. I mean, if the pair of us were biscuits, she'd be the Fox's chocolate round – delicious, really hits the spot, everybody's first choice – whereas I'd be the rich tea – plain, unappealing, only good if there's sod-all else. I must be stupid to believe that someone like Dan could live happily-ever-after with someone like me, although the optimist in me wants to believe that my husband's out-of-character behaviour is purely down to the stresses of parenthood. We have been living like roommates, after all, both engrossed in an endless routine of bottles and nappy changes. We've forgotten that we're lovers. Or, worst case scenario, Dan's been deliberately trying to forget that!

Though the twins are a blessing that I wouldn't change for the world, it's incredibly hard going. When something as simple as going for a piss has to be planned, what chance is there of going through the Kama Sutra? The last few months have been like a mini-tornado, and it seems the flames of pre-parenthood passion have all but blown out in it. Back in the days of my office crush on Dan, the idea of being fertilised by him was about as pathetic as I feel right now. Just brushing against his arm was enough to propel me to a lottery win high for the rest of the week, so you can only imagine how big a fantasy marriage and babies was.

Now I'm living the dream, except right now it's more a living nightmare as I sit in bits at the sight of the love of my life enveloped in the clutches of his tantalising boss. He's smiling, laughing, openly flirting, and I've never felt so small – or large for that matter – as I do looking at her slinky arse gliding about in that figure-hugging gold frock. Kill! Kill! Kill!

Well, there's absolutely nothing to be done here, short of marching over, slut-dropping and throwing angry shapes to Wham! in initiation of a weird, vengeful sort of festive dance-off.

Choked with anguish and with my worst fears all but confirmed, I rise shakily to my feet, make like a donkey's schlong and hit the road. Well, that was the intention, but somehow in my race to flee I trip over a chair leg and go flying for what seems like forever. Everything grinds to slow motion as I head for the deck, crashing on my side to the floor with a disorientating *thud*, bouncing, then bouncing again before skidding to an eventual stop.

Mortified, I freeze in position, peering around the huddle of surprised faces looking back at me, momentarily debating whether to laugh it off or burst into delayed tears in a toddler-like manner.

Well, don't all rush to help me at once, will you? Bastards!

Voice in head: *At least this isn't the Brit Awards. At least I'm not Madonna.*

Red-faced and mumbling self-soothingly, I scrabble to my feet as quickly as my throbbing lower limbs can manage it. Oh, fuck. Here comes Frank careering toward me, arms outstretched like a pervy scarecrow.

'What's oop, bab? Coome to Uncle Frankie!'

Voice in head: *Run, Forrest, run!*

Ducking beneath his hefty arms, I flee the ballroom in a sort of part limp, part run, sobbing at speed into the lobby and down the main entrance steps toward the orderly line of black, London cabs sat waiting outside the venue.

'Just take me home!' I sob, collapsing dramatically into the back of one of them.

'Sorry, love. I'm booked,' the driver replies from the front.

Ah, shit.

'Oh. Sorry, sorry!' I clamber out red-faced and hotfoot it into the next.

Mental note: *Well, this most definitely wasn't the wonderful night I thought we'd have! How could he do this to me? And her? I mean, hello! Girl code?! Well, that's it, I'm leaving!*

Follow-up note: *I'm already leaving.*

Like a depressed dog, I stare melancholically out the back of the rear window as the cab pulls away down the long driveway. The twinkling lights of the venue drift further and further into the distance, with Dan inside slow-dancing with the she-devil to my favourite Christmas song of all time. Shivering like the Little Match Girl, I slump down into my seat, briefly wondering if, like my hip, my marriage might be fucked. How has it come to this? I thought we had the fairy tale. The epic rainbow ending. But I suppose not all fairy tale endings are happy, and rainbows are just a trick of the light after all.

Chapter 16:

Baby it's Cold Outside

Waking to cold, undisturbed sheets beside me the next morning, my heart sinks as the first thought of the day hits. *Where did he sleep last night?*

Flipping back the bedcovers, I race to the front room, quite forgetting about my hip which immediately stops me in my tracks with expletive-inducing shooting pains. Limping the rest of the way into the sitting room, I begin to feel like Macaulay Culkin on finding the place empty and myself home alone. I mean, unless Dan's curled up on the sofa in Harry Potter's invisibility cloak, he didn't come home at all last night.

Voice in head: *He's with her! He stayed the night at hers! They made love into the early hours!*

Consumed by a carousel of images of them entwined in breathless ecstasy on sophisticated bed linen – all totally fabricated, of course, but nonetheless biblically unnerving – I collapse onto my knees and burst into tears.

It all should've been so simple. New job + mortgage + new house = happy-ever-after! But no. Why is fate so cruel? It's always the same old story with me. Just as I see my ship coming in, a fucking tsunami arrives out of nowhere to annihilate it. Of all the women in the world, why was *she* sent to test our marriage? I mean, why not send a five out of ten rather than an eleven out of ten? At least then I might've stood half a sodding chance!

A loud buzzing from the intercom startles me. Without thinking, I rise to my feet, race toward it and lift the receiver, then find myself unable to speak through my heaving great sobs.

'Lizzie?'

Dan. It's Dan!

'Lizzie, are you okay?'

Well, I've had better fucking days. Is he for real?!

'Let me come up, will you?' he pleads. 'It's gotta be around minus three out here and I'm bloody freezing!'

Frowning, I peer between the wooden slats of the blinds at the front window to find the street below covered in a blanket of fluffy snow. OMG, snow in December! How festively idyllic! My face lights up for all of five seconds, till I remember my marriage is in crisis and I'll probably be spending this Christmas lonelier than Mud ... or worse, with bloody Mother!

I give the button on the intercom a half-hearted *thwack*, hurriedly claw at my insane hair – even though it's all much too little too late – and hold my breath until a soft knock comes at the front door.

Dan gasps as I open the door, and I feel my face crumple at the mere sight of him. 'Lizzie, what on earth…'

Note to self: *Am exceedingly ugly crier. Must cease and desist, or at least try to keep face stationary.*

'W-well, we don't all look like H-Hollywood starlets f-first thing in the morning,' I wail.

'No, I mean you're in such a state.' He frowns in concern, ushering me inside the flat. 'Come here,' he mumbles, moving to hug me and jolting in surprise as I push him away.

'Don't touch me!'

'Whoa!' he exclaims, holding up his hands in surprise. 'Okay, I think we need to talk.'

I give a relenting nod and then perch timorously on the edge of the sofa.

An awkward clamour ensues as we both attempt to talk at once.

'You go,' he offers.

'No, you go.'

'Alright,' he mutters, clearing his throat. 'Look, Lizzie. Things haven't been the same since … well, since the twins were born,' he begins in a grave tone.

Mental note: *Shit. I've got that feeling. The one you get where you draw up two minutes too late at the drive-thru.*

'Surely you've felt it?' he continues.

I gulp. 'Yes.'

'Right.' He nods, solemnly. 'So what I'm about to say shouldn't come as a complete surprise to you then.'

'No. I've kn-known for a while,' I reveal, my mind turning over weeks' worth of little signs and clues.

'Oh?' he exclaims, appearing almost pleasantly surprised. 'So have you thought about what you'll do?'

'Sorry?' I gasp, glancing up at him in surprise.

Voice in head: *Wow. This is moving quickly! At least give me a chance to take this all in before we talk living arrangements!*

'I mean, what do you want to do?' he asks.

Well, other than tear you both limb from limb, I've not really thought about it!

'Well, there's not a lot I *can* bloody do, is

there?' I snort in disbelief.

'Don't be daft! These things happen to the best of people. You don't have to roll over and give up,' he counters sternly, an audacious eye roll following.

Wow, victim-blaming. Nice!

'Well, I don't know. What do you think I should do about it, Dan? Find a load of people who've had the same thing happen to them and sit comparing notes?' I yell, fast beginning to wonder if I ever actually knew this changed person in front of me whom I had thought I'd known inside-out.

'That could work.' He shrugs, catapulting me into a fit of rage.

'You're unbelievable!' I bawl in disbelief. 'What's happened to you?! You've changed! And it's all since you started that job working alongside those over-confident, self-absorbed arseholes with their oily combovers and free fucking fruit and … and stupid great slides in the workplace!'

His mouth falls open in disbelief. '*Me?!* I've changed? Tell me how I've changed?' he demands, furious.

'The Dan I knew would never do this. He would never have treated me how you did last night,' I part scream, part cry. 'You made me feel so small. So alone. So … unwanted!'

'Well you embarrassed me, Lizzie' he

reasons. 'Nobody else's wife was talking about the size of their shits at the dinner table.'

'Yeah, well, I'd had a lot of wine for my nerves,' I mumble in a low voice. 'And I only wanted to win them over. *Everybody* laughs at poo jokes, don't they?'

'If you're a five-year-old, yeah,' he mutters. 'But really, what did you expect from a bunch of executives?'

'Are we talking about the same executives who slide into the workroom every morning?' I ask, head wobbling in outrage.

'Alright. I'll let you off on that one,' he mumbles.

'Thank you.' I nod, drawing in a deep breath before going back in again. 'I tried my best, Dan. Even with everything going on and even when Amber deliberately separated us so that you could be together, I—'

'Sorry?!' he cuts in.

'Oh, don't play dumb! She fixed it so that you were sat next to each other and I was out the picture.'

He frowns. 'Why would she do that?'

'Well, I thought I was about to get that part from *you*,' I challenge, folding my arms, expectantly.

Silence.

'Well?' I probe, bracing myself for the confession I've been dreading for so long.

And then, he says it…

'Lizzie, I think it might help you to know that Amber's a lesbian.'

I freeze as a thousand party poppers go off in my head all at once. I must've misheard him. 'You what?!'

'She's gay,' he repeats. 'You remember the redhead sitting next to her at the table last night?'

'Yeah?'

'That was her wife, Helen.'

My mouth hangs open. Then closes. Then opens again. Fuck me, I must look like a puffer fish!

'But she deliberately sat us apart!' I pipe up, anxious that Mr Guns might be just the man to turn her straight.

'No, she didn't,' he snaps back. 'Apparently Frank was first at the table. We think *he* might've swapped the place cards.'

My mouth falls open in horror. 'Why would he do that?'

'Well, just as we were finishing up dessert, Amber mentioned that he's a bit weird. Has fetishes and that. Apparently he's into voluptuous women in a big way,' he explains, squinting suddenly in the direction of the sideboard. 'Er … did you open today's door on my advent calendar?'

Damn his x-ray vision!

'Er, yeah. I mean, I wasn't sure if you were coming home again,' I excuse in a mousey voice.

'What?! Why would I not be coming home again?' he snorts.

I wave my hand dismissively. 'Anyway, you were saying about Frank?'

Dan's face relaxes. 'Yes. Well, anyway, I thought I was coming to your rescue asking you to dance, but you'd hurt your foot and you seemed like you were okay in his company, so when Amber suggested she take your place, I just went along with it. I mean, she's gay. We're both married. You were resting your foot. Where's the harm?'

A long pause follows as I compute the aforementioned, my thinking accompanied by a series of surprised *ohhhs*, *ahhhs* and *hmmms* of varying pitch and tone.

'B-but she was so flirty with you,' I point out. 'And you never stop talking about her!'

'Lizzie, I talk about Amber all the time because she's an amazing boss,' he explains. 'She wasn't flirting. That's how she is with everyone. She's just a really friendly person and she treats us all like family. Come on, you saw the size of the cake she arranged for my birthday. I've never had that sort of treatment in any job I've worked before.'

'Well, she didn't treat *me* like family. In fact, I found her to be rude, actually,' I scoff, thinking back to that awful introduction in the bar. 'She barely acknowledged me when you first introduced us.'

'Only because she didn't see you till you stepped out,' he reasons, making it all sound like a scene from *The Wizard of Oz*.

'She called me Lydia!' I quickly cut in.

'So? Probably just down to the drink,' he excuses. 'She said she and Helen had a room booked at the hotel and they'd been drinking champagne since afternoon tea.'

'But she's stunningly beautiful! She could have any man she wants!' I blurt.

'Yes, but she doesn't *want* a man, Lizzie. She's gay.' Dan sighs, shaking his head. 'Tell me where it's written that lesbians can't be stunningly beautiful?'

'Oh. No. Yeah. Yes, of course, you're right,' I stammer, quickly collecting myself. 'I didn't mean to stereotype, it's just … she's every man's fantasy and I thought you were in love with her.'

He almost chokes. 'What?!'

'I thought you were planning to run off together!' I whimper with cow eyes. 'I've been going stir-crazy thinking you were with her every time you came home late from work. Honestly, Dan, I've been going out of my mind!'

'Well, that explains a few things,' he mumbles.

I look at him expectantly.

'I thought you might be suffering with post-natal depression,' he reveals softly. 'I was planning to talk to you about it. That's why I asked you what you wanted to do. I meant it in terms of getting you some help.'

'Oh. No. God, no!' I remark in surprise. 'I mean, I'm fine! I know it might not look like it sometimes, but I'm fine, honestly.'

We chuckle briefly at the crossed wires.

'So, where did you sleep last night?' I ask, after an awkward pause.

'In the car. I didn't have the keys on me, but I tried the door out of sheer desperation and luckily you'd forgotten to lock it after you went down to get your lip gloss out of the glove box yesterday afternoon.'

'Oh, God. Sorry, Dan. I've been way overdrawn at the memory bank lately.'

He chuckles sympathetically. 'Well, it paid off this once!'

'You must've been freezing! Why didn't you

call me?'

'I did,' he explains, 'but I sort of gave up after around the twentieth time of it going straight to voicemail. I assumed your battery was out because you only ever charge your phone when it dies on you. I keep telling you about that!'

'Oh. Yeah, it must be off then,' I mumble, feeling terrible that, rather than sizzling in his hot boss's bed like I'd envisioned, my poor husband was out in the car all along, freezing his gonads off. 'Why didn't you buzz?' I ask.

'I buzzed for ages, but you didn't answer.' He frowns, rolling his eyes.

'Oh. I must've nodded off quickly,' I say, thinking better of admitting to lying in bed, tears streaming and earphones in listening to podcasts about break-ups and divorce into the early hours!

'Listen, Dan. I'm sorry. I'm so sorry! I've behaved like an absolute arse and I just want you to know that I love you and I never should have doubted you and I'm sorry and … are we okay?' I plead.

Silence.

'Dan? Please tell me we're okay,' I repeat, bottom lip quivering.

He lets out a long sigh, head in hands.

Okay, that silence isn't good. Either this is an X-Factor *style build-up, or he's had enough of my shit once and for all.*

'Dan?' I sniff, holding my breath for his reply.

'Look, as far as I'm concerned, we were always okay. We were *better* than okay! My feelings for you have never changed,' he replies, looking up at me. 'I love you! Always have, always will. But you've really got to work on your self-esteem, babe. I've got to say, I'm pretty disappointed. Where's your trust in me? Do you know how it makes me feel to think that you've been sat here going out of your mind with worry that I must be cheating on you when all the while I've been going the extra mile to cinch deals and bag commission? And I'm doing it all for *you* Lizzie, for *us!* I'm working hard to build us a better future. To get us out of here and into our own place.'

'I know, I know! I'm so sorry, Dan. I appreciate everything you do for us, r-really I do,' I sob. 'But someone like you will never understand the fear of someone like me losing someone like you.'

'What?' He frowns, looking confused.

'Sorry. Didn't come out quite right,' I excuse, closing my eyes and drawing in a deep breath. 'Look, I saw your colleagues' faces when you introduced me as your wife,' I reveal. 'It's always been the same from the get-go every time we hold hands in public. Especially since I started putting the weight back on. The stares, the sniggers, the whispers that I don't need to even hear to know they're saying "What's someone like him doing with someone like her?"'

He sits shaking his head.

'To everybody else, we're a total mismatch. The most unlikely couple ever. People like *you* don't marry people like me, Dan. Attractive people marry attractive people. You're attractive and I'm near enough aesthetically bankrupt!'

'Hold on, let me get this straight. You're basically telling me attractive people can only be in relationships with similarly attractive people and vice versa? What a ridiculous theory!' he cuts in fiercely. 'You know I don't care about living up to other people's expectations. I live my life by my own playbook. Nobody's going to tell me who I should and shouldn't marry.'

'I know. It's just ... when you and Amber were dancing, you were like Barbie and Ken. I know she's gay, but I didn't know that then and even I could see you looked amazing together. Physically she's so much more on your level. She's just the type people would expect you to be with.'

'Yeah, well that's the difference between you and me, babe. I don't let other people write my story.' He sighs, rising from the sofa and beginning to pace the floor. 'Listen, when I married you, I married for love. Love doesn't discriminate. Your size is irrelevant to me. It's just the wrapping you come in. I'm in love with the person inside and I've told you that till I'm blue in the face,' he explains, melting my heart to mush. 'Too many people marry for the wrong reasons these days. Some for lust. Some for status. Some for money. Well, *they're* the ones who've got it wrong, Lizzie. Not me. As far as I'm concerned, I'm the happiest guy in the world!'

'Really?' I sob joyously.

'Absolutely! I know what I feel,' he says, turning to face me. 'Listen, I know things haven't exactly been white-hot in the bedroom department, but it's only because I've been wrapped up in work and I've been trying to be mindful about not putting any pressure on you because of how low you've seemed lately. You still do it for me, babe.' He smiles suggestively. 'You've *always* done it for me. Haven't I always said you're all woman?'

I nod, peering down at my Tweety Pie pyjamas still sporting yesterday's chocolate Ready Brek stain.

'Come here!' he orders with come-to-bed eyes.

'What, now?' I gulp in surprise.

'Why not? The twins aren't home. Let's make the most of it!'

'But … I've literally just fallen out of bed. I haven't even put a comb through my hair or—'

He storms over, lunges forward and kisses

me hard on the mouth without another word. 'Let's go back to bed, then,' he moans in my ear, leading me by the hand to the bedroom.

At last! It's been weeks. I've practically gone into administration down there!

Chapter 17:

This is Your Life

I blink and blink again at the shiny set of house keys I'm clutching in the palm of my right hand one year on from Christmas party-gate, not quite believing they're ours at last. The keys to number 10 Redfield Close, our three-bed, semi-detached new-build. Not only our dream house, but our forever family home. Ever since our first viewing several months ago, I've been hyperventilating about the place! So much so I've been getting Dan to drive me there every day while the sale's been going through, for no good reason other than to stare at it.

The mere second we draw up outside our brand spanking new home, and before the car wheels have even come to a complete stop, I whip my seatbelt off, bolt through the door and practically gallop up the front path. Aww, our path.

'Dan, look! Our path! Our very own path!' I beam, turning toward him. 'Don't you just love it? It's all new and concrete-y!'

He laughs, not quite matching my insane level of enthusiasm for what is probably to him just a load of concrete slabs. But they're ours! They're *our* concrete slabs!

'And our door! Our door! Look at it! All shiny and black! How amazing is our front door, Dan?' I grin, showcasing it like a gameshow hostess, as though it were the most desirable and sought-after door in the entire world.

'It's great.' He chuckles. 'Um, Lizzie, you're not going to be like this about every single fixture and fitting in the house, are you?' he mumbles quietly.

Practically foaming at the mouth, I slip the key into the lock and push the door open to be met with that wonderful smell of newness: new carpets, new woodwork, newly plastered and painted walls and … OMG, the kitchen! The kitchen!

'We have an island! We actually have an island, Dan!' I squeal, already picturing the untold hammerings we might enjoy on it – provided it'll take my weight, obviously.

When you've rented for what seems like an eternity, buying your own home is up there with winning the lottery. It's elation on a scale that only fellow renters can bear testimony to. I mean:

1. Carpets worth taking your shoes off for!
2. The lack of crap eighties wallpaper and mis-matched floral curtains!

3. An oven worth cleaning!
4. The pleasant lack of mould!
5. For cleaning efforts to actually pay off rather than leave you feeling as though you're pissing in wind!
6. A gleaming fridge that doesn't harbour a permanent, unidentifiable smell of farts!
7. Tile grout so perfect the shower curtain need not be fully drawn every time you're expecting visitors!

This is it! New beginnings! The closing of too long a chapter in my life wasted doubting my own happiness, feeling unworthy and undeserving of it because of what others think. I almost lost myself at the thought of losing Dan, my better judgement clouded by society's judgement of me. It left me feeling like an imposter in my own marriage, that all I had was meant for someone slimmer and prettier who pronounces their 't's' and doesn't eat yoghurts with a fork.

Slowly but surely I'm building my self-esteem. Which, by the way, turns out is *not* just for the aesthetically abundant, but for anyone who wants it. I haven't lost a pound in weight, but I'm light. I'm free of the weight of negativity that has been bearing down on me for so long. I'm learning that you don't have to be the best to win in life, and the winner isn't always the favourite. Every so often, the 100 - 1 shot comes in ... and here I am!

It's been a long time coming, but finally I'm accepting that, though I may be lightyears from perfect, I am worthy and I am enough. I am who I am, and who I am needs no apologies.

Finally, I'm writing my own story…

And here's my happy ending.

Epilogue:

Six months later...

Newham University Hospital antenatal clinic, East Ham.

'Okay, Mrs Elliott, you're going to feel some cold gel,' the sonographer warns in a cheery voice, smearing it over my bump.

Well, what can I say? All this new-found self-esteem has done wonders for our sex life! Okay, so the paint has barely had time to dry in our brand-new forever-home, and one of the twins will draw the short straw and have to share a bed-room with their new brother or sister, but it's no big deal. We'll get them some cool bunk beds! I always wanted bunk beds as a kid, but Mother said it was pointless since I was an only child. She denied me hours of playing pirate ships on the top bunk, as well as a handy alternative place to sleep on the odd occasion I'd pissed the bed.

'Right then, let's take a look and see what's

going on in there.'

I look to Dan in nervous anticipation, as the sonographer pushes the scanner firmly over my skin. He smiles back at me and gives my hand a little squeeze.

'Ah, there we are! A good, strong heartbeat!' she declares in a spirited tone. Then, in a decidedly less spirited tone, 'Oh … oh goodness. Just a second!'

Dan and I exchange worried glances while she sits frowning at the screen.

'What?! What is it? What's wrong?!' I gulp, fearing the worst.

'Oh, er. Nothing's wrong, sweetie. It's just that there appears to be *two* heartbeats.'

DUN-DUN-DUUUUN!

Mental note: *Unless am pregnant with Time Lord, this means am carrying twins. Again.*

I slowly turn to face Dan who, in five seconds flat, appears to have turned as white as a sheet.

'Looks like we're gonna need a bigger boat!'

About The Author

Gem Burman

Gem Burman is a British women's fiction writer from Norwich, UK.

www.gemburman.com

Books In This Series

A Kind of Tragic

A three-part romantic comedy fiction series following the catastrophic life and daily struggles of plus-sized, potty-mouthed Lizzie Bradshaw and her brutally honest and hilarious experience of singledom, unrequited love and beyond.

A Kind Of Tragic

She's the perfect poster girl for how not to be and what not to do in life. Every day is an epic fail with calamity around every corner. She's a dreamer. A schemer. A complete chancer, totally winging it with no life plan and just hoping everything will somehow work out... but who says you can't be the world's biggest ninny and still win?

Lizzie Bradshaw's two great loves in life are donuts and Dan Elliott, her devilishly handsome co-worker and hers is one brutally honest and hilarious account of unrequited love that you do not want to miss.

Guys like Dan Elliott wouldn't usually look twice at women like Lizzie, let alone date them. But what if there was a way to change the odds and turn fate on its head, even with the supermodelesque new starter at work also vying for Dan's affections? (Cow!) It all seems too good to be true, but sometimes, all is not as it seems and Lizzie might just be about to discover she can have her cake and eat it; in more ways than one!

Disclaimer: not suitable for prudes, puritans, sticks-in-the-mud, goody-goodies, and/or the easily offended. May cause laughter-induced bursts of incontinence.

Warning: Page-turner. Highly addictive. May need to put entire life on hold whilst reading.

A Kind Of Tragic Wedding

The date is set and the venue booked; everything in place for the nuptials of the future Mr & Mrs. Brian Garcia. But after a chance encounter with Dan Elliott (a.k.a Mr. Wonderful), what was all very simple and straightforward is now anything but!

Two love interests. Ninety-nine problems. One BIG decision ...

Lizzie Bradshaw is back!

Printed in Great Britain
by Amazon